Doing My Part

Also by Teresa R. Funke

Dancing in Combat Boots
and Other Stories of American Women
in World War II

Remember Wake

Visit www.teresafunke.com to:

• Add your stories or your family's stories
about the past.

• Learn more about kids'
experiences in World War II.

• Find out how to schedule Teresa
to speak at your school.

To Sasha—

Doing My Part

Enjoy!

Teresa Funke

Teresa R. Funke

VICTORY
HOUSE
PRESS

Published by:

Victory House Press
3836 Tradition Drive
Fort Collins, Colorado 80526
www.victoryhousepress.com

Library of Congress Control Number 2009936550

Printed in Canada

ISBN 978-1-935571-10-0
(Previously published by Bailiwick Press, ISBN 978-1-934649-01-5)

To my children, Brian, Lydia, and Ava,
who inspire me every day

Acknowledgments

I'd like to start by thanking my friend and fellow writer Laura Resau for suggesting I read a children's book called *Esperanza Rising* by Pam Muñoz Ryan. After finishing that wonderful novel, I got the urge to write my own stories for children. Then along came Joanie Ellis, a fifth grader at McGraw Elementary School in Fort Collins, who invited me to speak to her class about writing and World War II. She and her classmates showed such interest in the war and asked such wonderful questions that I then knew what my children's books should be about.

Then I'd like to thank my friends: the members of my writers group, The Slow Sand Writers Society, for assuring me I was on the right track during those early drafts; Victoria Hanley, who gave comments on the finished book; and Lisa Spires and Susan Skog, who showered me with encouragement.

Then I'm happy to thank my children: Brian and Lydia, who read the first draft of this novel and told me honestly how much they liked it, but also a few ways I could improve it; and Ava, who asked me often how the book was coming along and when she'd be able to read it. And, of course, I have to thank my husband, Roger, for taking me to Vancouver, Washington the week of my birthday so I could write most of this book, and who always, always supports me.

And then there's my writing partner, Karla Oceanak, who knew years ago I could write a children's book and helped me not only edit, but design and publish *Doing My Part*. I couldn't have done it without her. And special thanks to Kendra Spanjer and Launie Parry for creating such a wonderful cover and my daughter, Lydia, for serving as the model for the cover image.

But I especially need to thank Shirley Brand, the woman on whose life this book is based. If Shirley had never told me her stories about growing up in a small Illinois town during World War II, this book would not exist. You never know what wonderful stories are awaiting you until you ask, so go ahead, ask someone today for their story, and if you feel the urge, write it down!

1

The 4:30 Train

The sun's not up yet, my breakfast hasn't settled, and already I'm running. Janie's falling farther behind. "Hurry up," I yell, but rushing Janie only makes her slip more on the dew-wet grass, which starts her giggling. Janie doesn't care if we miss the train to work, but I do. I need this job. I can hear the train whistle echoing down the valley and it makes me want to sprint the last stretch to the depot. But Janie drops her lunch sack and laughs all the harder.

"Oh come on, Janie. It's not funny."

"It is to me, Helen."

"Everything's funny to you. The way you act, no one would know there's a war on."

She's making a face at me—I know it—but it's too dark to see which one.

"And how do you expect me to keep up with those long legs of yours, anyway?"

I cringe. My legs are longer than any girl's in Hayden's Valley. In fact, there's hardly a man in the state of Illinois taller than me, and I'm only fourteen. Every night I pray that I'm done growing. I can't stand the thought of dancing with a man shorter than me, and I won't marry a man who can't dance. Thinking such thoughts slows my pace, and Janie catches up to me easily.

"Oh quit your brooding." She nudges me gently with her shoulder. "There are worse things in life than being tall. At least *you* don't still have freckles." She locks arms with me, and we walk together along the railroad tracks.

Janie Brey's a grade above me in school. She's been my best friend since Mother and I moved here to live with my grandparents after my dad died. She's the one who talked me into applying for work at the Westclox factory ten miles away in the town of Peru. Before the war, Westclox was famous for its alarm clocks and watches. Now it's a war plant. Janie wanted to do her part for the war effort, and she wanted me to come with her. I didn't think they'd hire me because I'm too young, but the supervisor took one look at my height and didn't notice on my application that I won't actually be fifteen until October. At first I was just glad to be with Janie, but now that Mother has been injured and can't work, my family is counting on *me* to bring home the paycheck.

The whistle blows again, louder this time, but we're not far now. I can smell the earthy scent of the geraniums my grandmother helped plant around the depot. I'm glad the 4:30 train is on time this morning. Yesterday it was more than two hours late, and I grew so impatient I kicked a post, stubbing my toe. Janie offered me no pity. She hates it when I lose my temper. She doesn't understand, though. If we're late to work, they dock our pay. That doesn't matter much to Janie. She'll be spending the money she earns this summer on frivolous things like clothes and hair curlers. I had fun plans for my money too. I've had my heart set on a plaid wool jacket and matching skirt I saw in the Sears Roebuck catalog. But a few nights ago I overheard Grandpa George, Grandma Kate and Mother discussing Mother's medical bills. They thought I'd gone to bed.

"It's not just the extra bills, Papa," Mother was saying. "We have to fix the roof this fall, and Helen needs new shoes and a good winter coat."

"I could take in some sewing," Grandma Kate offered.

"Oh Mama, you have your hands full around here."

"We expanded the garden this spring, so we should have enough vegetables. I suppose we could even trade a few vegetables for eggs and maybe a little meat," Grandpa George said. "Helen's paycheck should be enough to cover the rest."

"If she makes it through the summer," Mother said.

It stung a little to hear her say that. Of course I'd make it through the summer! But I couldn't fault Mother for wondering. She was worried. For years now, ever since Grandpa's arthritis in his hands has gotten so bad he can't take on handyman jobs anymore, Mother has been supporting our family.

"She'll make it," Grandma Kate said.

Her comment kind of surprised me. Though I know she loves me, Grandma's more likely to lecture than praise. This was as near to a compliment as anything I'd heard from her lately, and it filled me with pride.

"Well, I don't want her knowing any of this. She's too young to have to carry so much responsibility," Mother said.

"She can handle it," Grandpa George replied. And ever since I heard him say it, I've been out to prove I can.

We get to the depot just as the train is arriving. The conductor raises an eyebrow and snaps his pocket watch closed. I wonder if that watch was made at Westclox before the war, and then I remember something I heard once, that railroad men often pass down their timepieces from father to son, generation after generation. I don't know if it's true or not, but I like to think so. I have nothing of my father's except the violin he used to play for me when I was little.

As the train rocks forward, we ease past a rail-thin man in shirtsleeves and suspenders and squeeze up next to the window. We sit real close to each other, making ourselves as small as possible, glad for the skinny man beside us. His size means Janie won't need to sit on my lap this morning. All the passenger trains are crowded these days because there are fewer of them. Many are troop trains now, and regular folk, like my family, are supposed to try not to travel. No one worries about our discomfort so long as the soldiers get where they need to go. Everything we do now is for them. If they don't beat the Germans and the Japanese, we're in a world of trouble. I try not to think about that too much.

Janie cups both hands around my left ear and whispers, "I saw John Beaumont at church last night. Didn't you think he looked dashing in his uniform?"

I roll my eyes. Janie's had a crush on my cousin John since she was ten years old. He joined up in April, the very day he turned eighteen. Several of the senior boys have done that, strutting down to the recruiting station with their parents tagging behind. The parents wait outside—the fathers turning their hats in their hands, the mothers wiping away tears—while their sons enlist. A couple of boys have even signed up at age seventeen with their parents' permission. Mother told Grandma if she had a son, she'd keep him home as long as possible. I guess maybe those boys just couldn't wait to get into the fight.

"Why is John back?" Janie asks.

"He's home on leave to say good-bye. He finished his training. He'll be shipping out soon to be a flight navigator on an airplane."

"Well, he looked awfully dreamy in his dress uniform."

Janie looks away. I know she's trying to fix that picture of John in her mind so she doesn't forget it. It's early June 1942, and the war has been going on for six months. Our little town hasn't lost a single boy yet. We're all hoping John won't be the first. I try to picture my lanky cousin, who loves comic books and funny radio shows, doing anything as serious as helping fly a plane. When he arrived home the other day, he took his new silver wings off his uniform and pinned them on my blouse and said, "Helen, if you were a boy, you could get a pair of these for yourself." I wasn't sure if I wished I was a boy or not.

"Whatcha thinking about?" Janie asks.

"John. I'm wondering if he ever worries about getting killed. You've seen the newsreels, what it looks like when a plane gets hit. How it spins down toward the earth trailing a line of smoke behind it. Don't you think that'd be an awful way to die? Such a long way down."

"You shouldn't think things like that," Janie snaps.

She's right, of course, but how can I help it? I wonder if John thinks those thoughts. If he worries about dying. He doesn't seem to. He seems excited to leave, like this is all one big adventure. But that's just John. Everything is a game to him, and he always wins at games.

I take Janie's hand and squeeze it. "Don't worry. John was the toughest kid in school and the smartest. He can take care of himself." When I say it, I really believe it. I can see by the look in Janie's hazel-yellow eyes that she's trying to believe it too.

The sun is coming up and its rays are working their way through the dirty window. The humidity is rising, and it's getting stuffy in the train. The woman across from us has her chin tilted up and is fanning her neck with a copy of *Ladies' Home Journal.* I wish I'd thought to bring a magazine too. Then I get an idea that takes my mind off the heat. "Hey, Janie, maybe you should write to John."

Her face brightens. "Should I?"

"Sure."

"It could be like in the movies. I could be the girl he dreams about back home."

"Oh nausea," I say, which starts us both giggling. The skinny man next to us tosses us a disapproving glance, then tips his head back and closes his eyes, pretending we're not there. We lean into each other and laugh even harder as the train rattles on toward Peru.

2

Westclox

I love the Westclox factory. It's not like other factories, at least not from the front. It's much prettier, with its three stories of dark red brick and decorative iron work and its Big Ben clock above the main entrance. The factory has been around since the 1880s, and nearly everyone in the Illinois Valley knows someone who works at Westclox. They live in LaSalle or Peru or drive in from the smaller towns. Or like Janie and me, they take the bus or the train. My own grandmother worked for a year at Westclox when she was younger, though she doesn't talk about it much.

"It was just something I did for the extra money," she says.

Like Grandpa, Grandma's always known

her place, and her place is at home. I don't share that feeling, though. I like the excited rush of the traffic on 5th Street as we walk up to the factory's double doors, the crush of hundreds of men and women arriving for work, the *chunk-chunk* sound of timecards punching in. I even like the slam of all those metal locker doors where folks store their wraps and lunches. It's the sound of people heading off to work.

After we put our things in our lockers, Janie moves on upstairs. She's assigned to a different department than I am. At least for now. I'm replacing a woman who's taking some time off to care for her daughter's new baby. I'll be at this spot for a few weeks, if not the whole summer.

I make my way down a long hall and into a cavernous room filled with rows of long tables that make up the assembly lines. The other women, all of them older than me, take their seats up and down the line. Betty is to my left and Martha to my right. Rita sits across from me, and she is the only one I smile at. Martha and Betty have made it clear they don't like me. It appears they don't like anyone but each other. I figure if I pay them no mind, maybe they'll leave

17

me alone.

But it's not me they're after today, it's Rita. I know this as soon as they make a comment about the dark circles under her eyes and start to tease her.

"You're looking a bit over-tired today, Rita," Betty says. "Don't you know a bride's supposed to look her best?"

"What's the matter, Rita? Did you stay up all night worrying your fiancé won't show up for the wedding?" Martha asks.

It's a cruel joke. Rita's fiancé joined the navy in the spring. They're supposed to get married next week when he's home on furlough, and Rita has been spending all her free time getting ready for the wedding. That's the reason she looks so tired. Betty and Martha know that, but they keep teasing her just the same.

I pull my stool up close to my drill press and wait for the first timing device to make its way down the line to me. Someday soon that device will be fixed to a bomb and will travel halfway round the world to do its job against the Nazis or the Japs. I think about that often as I take the pieces shaped like little wooden tops off the moving belt and fix them on the peg of my drill. I pull the handle and bring down the drill bit in exactly the right place for the hole, then I raise the bit, remove the timing device, and put it back on the belt, where it moves on down to Betty. I'll do this all day and I won't mind a bit, even when it gets so hot my blouse sticks to my back and not even the large, heavy fans keep us cool anymore. It makes me proud to think I'm doing my part to help us win the war. I don't have silver wings like John, but I have my Westclox badge.

I'm working as hard as I can, though I can only be as fast as the women before and after me, and those are Martha and Betty. They are both in their thirties or forties and have been at Westclox forever. Martha is small in stature, but she makes up for it by talking louder than she needs to and waving her arms so she takes up more space. Betty is younger than Martha, but she looks older. Her brown hair is streaked with grey, and there are deep lines around her eyes. My mother calls those "laugh lines," and Betty does laugh a lot, but mostly at other people. She favors polka-dots. Nearly every dress she owns has a polka-dot pattern. Betty and Martha were nice to me when I started here last week, but that quickly changed.

"This company runs on quotas," Martha said.

"You know what that means?" Betty asked.

"Not exactly."

"It means the supervisors of each division look at how many pieces are produced in a certain day, and that's how they decide how many we should get done *every* day."

"So people like you who try to work too fast can raise the quota, which means the rest of us will have to work faster too," Betty said.

"And that's not something we want, is it?" Martha asked.

I wasn't sure at first how to answer. I thought maybe she was kidding. Why wouldn't anyone want to do the best job they could, I wondered? But she didn't leave me wondering for long.

"Slow. . . down," she warned, bringing her pinched face in close to mine.

I did slow down too. For the rest of the day anyway. Then I got angry. It was wrong for them to be slowing down war work and wrong for them to be trying to scare me. I considered talking to Mother about it, but I didn't want her calling my supervisor.

Grandpa George always says it's best to ignore bullies, so that's exactly what I've been trying to do—ignore Martha and Betty. They don't talk to me much anymore, but they make it obvious they mean to distract me any way they can.

At the moment, though, they are focused on Rita.

Martha raises her voice above the whines and rattles of the fans and machinery. "Say, Betty," she says. "You know about sailors, right?"

"Oh sure. My cousin married herself one of those. Once a man gets a taste for the sea, he never comes home."

"So I've heard," Martha says, waving her arm in Rita's direction. "'Course that might not be the way with Rita's fella. Maybe he *will* come back. That is if the Japs don't get him first."

Rita shoves her stool back so hard it topples over, and she rushes off crying. The line stops almost immediately, which is exactly what Martha and Betty wanted. Another woman goes after Rita. Betty chuckles, and I feel a heat rising in me that has nothing to do with the temperature. But I don't say anything. I just fiddle with a loose button on my blouse. I feel bad for Rita, of course, but not bad enough to draw attention to myself. I'm not proud of that, but until I figure out how to sort this whole thing out, I'm better off laying low. Martha and Betty are my mother's age, and even if I wanted to confront them, I wouldn't know how. I glance around for our foreman, Mr. Mueller, but he's nowhere in sight. He's never where he's supposed to be. So I fiddle with my button some more and wish the line would just start moving again so I can do my job.

Rita isn't gone for long. She pulls herself together quickly and gets back to her seat. Martha throws her arms up in resignation, and Betty mutters under her breath, but the line starts moving and doesn't stop again until we break for lunch. I look up at Rita every now and then, trying to catch her eye, but she keeps her head low. She looks more tired than ever.

At four o'clock, my workday is done. I meet Janie in the lobby, and we walk a mile to the bus stop to catch a ride back to Hayden's Valley. The bus leaves earlier than the afternoon train. I tell Janie what Martha and Betty did to Rita, and she shakes her head. "Why are those two so mean?" she asks.

"Rita says Betty was married once, but her husband left her and that soured her on life."

"What about Martha?"

"Oh she's just ornery. Grandpa says some folks are just born mean. It's as much a part of their make-up as the color of their hair. I guess that's Martha."

"Well, I think you should tell your foreman."

"I would if I could find him."

"What do you mean? Doesn't he walk the line now and then?"

"Not more than once or twice since I've been there. In the morning I sometimes see him dozing in the corner. In the afternoon, he disappears for long stretches. They say he's gambling in the men's bathroom." I shouldn't repeat something I heard only from Betty, but I'm frustrated now and I don't care what I say.

"Honestly!" Janie says. "It's a wonder he's kept his job."

I consider this for a moment. "I guess they have no choice," I say. "With so many men off to war, maybe there aren't enough good men to work as foremen."

"Well, even I could do a better job than him," Janie says as we arrive at the bus stop. I pull her aside so no one can hear us.

"It's not what I expected, Janie. I thought working at Westclox would seem so grown up. But these people don't act grown up at all. I don't know if I like this job."

"Just wait, Helen. You'll get used to it. You'll see. Don't quit on me now. Not because of a couple of old cows."

I laugh in spite of myself. I don't remind Janie that I can't quit no matter how bad things get. My family needs me now, at least until Mother can get back to work, and I'm not about to let them down.

Janie changes the subject. She starts going on again about the floral dress with matching handbag she wants to order when she gets her paycheck. Maxine Land has one just like it, and Janie thinks Maxine is the height of fashion in our small town. I'm only half-listening, though. I'm still thinking about Betty and Martha. It's gonna be a long summer if I don't figure out how to deal with those two. But how?

3

Mrs. Osthoff

A few days later, the bus drops me off downtown after work, and I wave good-bye to Janie. I have just enough time to get to Anderson Hardware before they close to buy the Mixmaster for Grandma Kate. I got my first two-week paycheck today for fifty-five dollars, and not even Martha or Betty could ruin my excitement. I've been holding my paycheck tightly the whole way home, afraid it might blow away or fall out of my pocket and slip under the seat. All day long I've been thinking about that Mixmaster. Grandma Kate looks at it every time we go into the store. She runs her hand along its smooth, white surface and sighs. I know she wants it, though she'd never buy it for herself. I'm going to get it for her as an early birthday present.

"Good evening, Mr. Anderson," I say, a little out of breath. "I want to buy that Sunbeam Mixmaster."

"Do you now?" He grins. Mr. Anderson has always liked me. He says I remind him of his daughter, but I can't really. We both have chestnut-colored hair and brown eyes, but she's *much* prettier than I am.

"May I buy it on credit?" I ask. "I can pay you back as soon as I get to the bank to cash my check."

"Credit, huh? Well, I suppose I could start you an account in your own name. I can trust you, can't I?"

He's teasing, but I know he wants me to answer him anyway. "You sure can, Mr. A."

I'm positively full of myself as I leave the store, carrying the mixer in its box with the picture facing out so everyone will know what I bought. Grandma Kate does most of the baking in our house. In fact, she does most of everything, and she's always telling me I don't help out as much as I should. Maybe this will make up for that.

I'm balancing the box carefully to keep it safe, but I nearly drop it when Hal runs up behind me and pinches my sides. He steps in front of me, barring my way and grinning like a king's fool.

"Hal, you idiot," I say. "Can't you see I'm holding something?"

Hal is Janie's brother. He's older than her by a little more than a year. I like him, when he's not acting up. I like the way he lays his arm across my shoulders, as if I were his sister too, and says, "Hiya, Lanie." He's the only one who calls me that.

"Oh come on, Lanie," he says, pushing up his glasses. "No harm done. Here, let me carry that."

He takes the box, paying no attention to what's inside it. I wish he would ask me what I bought so I can tell him how I used my own money, but he doesn't. He's wearing his blue, striped coveralls, and he must have just finished his shift pumping gas at the station. He's worked there every summer since he was my age, so maybe making money doesn't seem so special to him anymore.

We talk about lots of things as we turn down Jefferson Street.

"Gerald Schultz joined up this morning," Hal says.

"He did?"

"Yeah, and Cindy Wittman is getting married."

"But she just turned seventeen!"

"Well, lots of girls are thinking about it. Pretty soon their boyfriends will all be gone, so they gotta marry 'em now," Hal explains.

"And all this happened today?" I ask.

"Yep."

"I'm missing everything," I groan.

"Well, that's the life of a working girl."

As we're cutting down the alley that runs behind my house, Hal is telling me about the box of Hershey's bars Mr. Simms has locked in a closet in the service station. Since they started rationing chocolate, a Hershey's bar has become a precious thing. I'm about to ask if there's any way Hal can sneak us one when I hear it — a high, piercing wail I've heard a dozen times before. It's not like any sound a human would make, yet it has to be human. It's coming from the open back window of Mrs. Osthoff's house. There's a short pause and then a long, low moan that pushes me closer to Hal. I grip his upper arm.

He looks at me, his eyes blinking quickly behind his thick lenses. "Come on," he says, leading me forward.

I unlatch my backyard gate and hold it open with

my hip as I take the box from him.

"You know what they say about her, don't you?" he asks.

"Who?"

"Mrs. Osthoff. They say she's a recluse. She never, ever leaves her house. Not even to get food."

"Oh Hal, that can't be true."

He leans in closer. "Toby Willis says she cries like that because she killed her husband and his spirit torments her."

I hug the box tighter and look hard into Hal's eyes. After a moment, he breaks our gaze and laughs. "You're such a scaredy-cat," he says.

If my hands weren't full, I'd hit him. As much as I like Hal, I hate being teased. It comes from being an only child, I suppose, not having older brothers and sisters to tell me tales and play tricks on me. I like to think I'm above that sort of thing. "Honestly, Hal. You're such a child," I say.

He laughs at me again and lets the gate bang shut as he jogs back down the alley. As he passes Mrs. Osthoff's house, he throws out an arm, shuddering like some invisible force is pulling him toward her house. I shake my head, though I can't help smiling just a bit. All is quiet now. The yellow curtains inside Mrs. Osthoff's window are fluttering out into the breeze, but no sound is escaping. Now that I think about it, though, I've never heard much about Mrs. Osthoff's husband or how he died, and it does make me wonder.

I carry the box up to the porch and catch my toe under the screen door to pull it open. I wipe my feet and cross the screened-in porch to the back door, which is standing open. I see my grandmother bustling around the kitchen getting dinner ready. Mother is sitting at the table, a recipe book propped open in front of her, her arms in casts. A little over a week ago she was coming down the stairs at the zinc plant where she works when she lost her footing and fell forward. She put her arms out to stop her fall and broke both of her wrists. The doctor says it will take at least ten weeks for the bones to heal, which is most of the summer.

Mother jokes that if she'd known all she had to do was break a few bones to get a summer off, she'd have done it years ago, but she doesn't mean it.

It's hard for her being unable to work or even help around the house. It's harder still thinking she's a burden to Grandma Kate, who now must help her do even simple things like bathe and dress. There was never a better time, I realize, to bring a Mixmaster home, and before I know it, I'm bursting into the kitchen yelling, "Surprise!"

"Merciful heavens," Grandma Kate scolds. "Haven't I told you not to yell in this house?"

"What have you got there?" Grandpa George asks as he comes in from the dining room. He was tall once, like me, but his shoulders are stooped now and his knees bent, as if his weight is almost too much for him. But his eyes are a clear blue, and his hair is still thick, with hints of dark brown showing through the grey. And he's still the smartest man I know. Grandpa is a good ten years older than Grandma, and the arthritis in his hands gets worse every year. He does what he can, but he spends most of the day reading the newspaper and listening to the radio. As bad as the war is, at least it has given Grandpa something to do. He follows it in detail and reports on it throughout the day, though sometimes I think Grandma wishes he wouldn't, and sometimes I wish he wouldn't either. I don't like to think about the war.

"I got you something," I tell Grandma. "For your birthday."

She cocks her head and looks at me sideways, like she does when she thinks I'm up to something. She's tall too—I definitely get my height from Mother's side of the family—and very thin, probably because she never stops moving. She wipes her hands on her apron and approaches the box cautiously. She turns it around and studies the picture on the side, then inspects it as if she's looking for something wrong. I grin at Mother, who stands up slowly and moves closer to her mother. "Are you going to open it, Mama?" she asks.

"Should I?"

There's a long pause, and I realize everyone is thinking about the money I spent, and now I'm thinking about it too, wondering if I made a mistake. But then Grandpa George speaks up. "Of course you should open it, Kate. It wouldn't do to hurt your granddaughter's feelings."

When Grandma still hesitates, my words rush out. "I know you've been wanting one, Grandma. It'll make things easier now that Mother can't help you cook and I'm working all day. And it's not so much money, really. It's . . ." I look down.

Grandma Kate lifts my chin gently. I can see in her eyes she's still a little worried, but then her face goes soft. "I wouldn't dream of taking it back, Helen. It's a wonderful gift. Here now, help me get it out of the box, George."

While Grandpa helps Grandma, I pull Mother aside and show her my paycheck, eager to redeem myself.

"Would you look at that?" she says with tears in her eyes. "Did you know you're making more than I do at the plant! Oh I wish I could hug you, you sweet girl."

I rest my head lightly on her shoulder, and she lowers her own head down on mine, and it's almost as good as a hug. Grandma pushes aside the bread box and moves the coffee pot to make room for the Mixmaster. Its shiny white surface stands out new and sleek against the speckled, grey counter. Grandma stands back for a moment to admire her gift, then rounds us all up with a clap and herds us into the dining room, where she's already set the table.

"You sit," she says to me. "I'll put the food out tonight."

This I can't believe. Helping put the food on the table has been my responsibility since I was a little girl.

"But you *will* help me clean up," Grandma adds, with a tap on my shoulder.

As we dish up our dinner, I talk excitedly about how I plan to cash the check the first chance I get and give the rest of the money to Mother. I tell them how I almost dropped the mixer thanks to Hal, and Grandma says that boy doesn't use the sense God gave him.

Then it gets quiet for a moment as everyone cuts into the duck that Grandpa shot this morning, everyone except Mother, who ate before I got home. I'm still so wound up that I don't think before I ask, "Grandpa, is it true that Mrs. Osthoff killed her husband?"

Grandpa's fork clanks down hard against his plate. They're all staring at me now. "Helen Faye Marshall," Mother says, "I'm surprised at you."

My cheeks burn. "I just thought . . ."

I can say no more. In fact, I wish I'd never said

anything at all. The mood is spoiled now, and it's all my fault. Mine and Hal's.

Grandma Kate picks up the bread basket and takes it back into the kitchen for more rolls. I risk a glance at Grandpa, who is wiping his mouth with his napkin. He clears his throat and asks, "Have you ever seen Mrs. Osthoff, Helen?"

"No, sir."

"Fine looking woman, wouldn't you say, Barbara?"

"Yes, Papa. Calvin used to say she looked like that old movie star, Lillian Gish." Mother's voice perks up, as it always does when she talks about my father. "'Course it's been many months since I've seen Mrs. Osthoff."

Grandma returns with more rolls, and Grandpa reaches for one. As he pulls it apart, the steam rises up and drifts across his weathered face. "Mrs. Osthoff came here with her husband as a young woman, Helen. She'd led a hard life in Germany. She's always been a homebody, but that doesn't make her strange. She just never saw the need to go out much, and she never learned more than a few words in English. Her husband, Otto, spoke English very well, though. He took care of everything for her."

"What happened to him?"

"He caught pneumonia one winter and died," Grandpa says. "After that, Mrs. Osthoff's son, Frederick, was her ticket to the outside world."

When Grandpa says his name, I suddenly remember Frederick. He was older than me by ten years at least, but he used to cross into our yard when I was little and push me on the tree swing. He wasn't much of a talker, I recall. Must have been shy, like his mother, but I do remember he was kind-looking, with dark, wavy hair and a soft smile. "Where is Frederick now?"

"He left when you were seven," Mother answers. "No one's sure why. Some say he went off to college. He was always a smart boy. Others say he had a falling out with his mother and left home. Still others say he met a girl on the train coming home from LaSalle and never got off, just rode on with her to a new life."

Grandma huffs. "That's a romantic notion, Barbara, but not very practical."

I mix my peas into my mashed potatoes, though I know Grandma hates that. I don't look at her in case she's glowering at me. I look straight at Grandpa George instead and say, "Is that why Mrs. Osthoff cries so much? She's missing her son?"

"It's none of our business why that poor woman cries," Grandma interrupts. "And that's quite enough of this conversation, young lady. I won't have gossip and speculation at my dinner table."

I risk a glance at Mother, hoping for support, but she's looking down, which means she's letting Grandma have her way.

We eat in silence for a moment, and then Grandpa says, "So what do you think, Helen? Will the corn be knee-high by the Fourth of July?"

I sigh. Next to the war, the corn crops are Grandpa's favorite subject. He owned a farm before his health turned, and he and Grandma sold it to move into town. In his heart, though, he'll always be a farmer. I know he wishes I'd take an interest, but other than the sweet smell the corn lends the summer air, I have no use for it, even though I know it's how many folks around here make their living.

While Grandpa drones on about the amount of rain the farmers will need soon, my own thoughts turn back to Mrs. Osthoff. I wasn't exactly truthful when I told Grandpa I'd never seen her. I'm not sure why I said that, except maybe I worried Grandma would think I'd been spying. It's nothing like that, though. I've happened to see Mrs. Osthoff a few times on those nights when my dreams wake me up and I go to my bedroom window to study the stars and think about what they mean. Mrs. Osthoff sometimes comes down her back steps in her nightdress and robe after most everyone is asleep, and gazes up at the night sky for a minute. I think she closes her eyes to feel the breeze on her face, though I can't see well enough from this distance to say for sure. Then she bends over a small garden she grows near the house, working only from the light from her kitchen window, which she shouldn't have on most nights because of the blackout rules.

She never stays out long, and she keeps her back to me all the while, yet somehow I've always felt she knows I'm there. Every time she goes back inside, she pauses on her top step, one hand on the screen door handle, and looks slightly over her right shoulder. I always shrink back a little from the window, thinking she's looking at me. Then she goes quietly inside, so quietly that I can almost forget she's the same

woman who lets loose those high, piercing screams
that sometimes shatter my dreams.

4

Hal's Secret

A couple of weeks later, Mother, Janie and I are talking excitedly in the movie theater, waiting for the four o'clock show to start. We know we'll have to endure the newsreels first. Unlike Grandpa George, I try not to think about the war too much, except to wonder how John is doing and to see if he will answer the letter Janie wrote. Sometimes I find the newsreels interesting, especially the ones about the Hollywood stars like Bette Davis or Clark Gable giving their all to the war effort. Other times they're too hard to watch. Not a showing goes by when you don't hear someone in the theater sniffling or even crying during the worst of the footage. We all know too many men fighting in the war now. It's too close to home.

I can stand the pictures of burning cities and bombed-out buildings. I can even stand the scenes of artillery firing at enemy ships or planes—though I hate to see the planes come down because it reminds me of John—but I can't stand the pictures of the starving people or the way the children in those torn-up countries look into the camera with hollow eyes. That's when I look away.

But today, even I am interested in the news footage. Mrs. Fuller, who lives next door to Mrs. Osthoff, says she saw a soldier in this week's newsreel who looks exactly like Frederick, Mrs. Osthoff's son. He's wearing a helmet and is seen only from the side, but she's sure it's him. He appears only for a second, in a clip that shows soldiers boarding a transport ship, so she said to watch for it carefully.

The newsreel starts with that booming voice of the commentator. Newsreel commentators always have booming voices. Janie and I have scooted to the edge of our seats and are staring intently at the flickering images. Even Mother is leaning forward, her hands resting carefully in her lap. After only a minute, we get to the clip.

"There it is," Janie shouts.

41

"Was it him, Mother? Was it Frederick?"

Mother's face is screwed up in concentration. "It's hard to say, Helen. It went by so fast. But it certainly did look like him."

I hear a strange sound, almost like a muffled gasp, and from the corner of my eye I see someone rise and walk quickly up the dark aisle. I turn just as a woman is disappearing through the heavy curtain leading to the lobby. I wonder if it could be Mrs. Osthoff, if just this once she has left her house, to see her son. I tell Mother I'm going to the bathroom, and I hurry up the aisle, but the lobby is empty and so is the street outside. Whoever it was, she was moving pretty fast.

We watch the feature *Yankee Doodle Dandy*. Mother cries a couple of times. She always cries in movies, especially the sentimental ones. Jimmy Cagney is one of my favorite actors and the show is so good that I almost forget about Frederick, but when we step outside, Mrs. Fuller is waiting anxiously by the curb. She says she's come to offer Mother a ride home, but I think she just wants to know what Mother thought. The whole town is starting to buzz about Frederick.

"I believe it *was* him," Mother says. "It was strange to see him looking so scruffy and tired. Frederick was always so careful about his appearance. Such a handsome boy. Seeing him walking up the plank toward that transport ship made it all seem so final, didn't it? It's still so hard to picture these boys as soldiers."

Mrs. Fuller doesn't give Mother's comment a second thought. "Imagine that," is all she says. "A boy from our own little town showing up in a newsreel. It's quite exciting, don't you think?"

Mother mumbles something in response and turns to ask if Janie and I want a ride home, but I tell her no. It's Saturday night and there's no early morning train to catch tomorrow. Janie and I are heading out toward the lake.

"Fine," she says. "But be home by dark."

Janie and I lock arms and sing "Yankee Doodle" in our best Jimmy Cagney voices as we dance off down Main Street. It rained while we were in the movie theater, cooling things off and lifting the humidity a bit, which should help my hair. The more humid the air, the more unruly my hair becomes. This time last summer, I got a permanent, but it made my hair as bushy as a squirrel's tail. I was so embarrassed I barely left my house for a week. My hair is certainly not my best feature, and I'm smoothing it down now as we head toward the edge of town, trying to make it behave.

"I think I saw Mrs. Osthoff in the theater," I say.

"Crazy Mrs. Osthoff!"

"Mother says she isn't crazy. She's just sad because she lost her family."

"Hal says she eats cats."

"Why on earth would he say that?"

"Because so many cats go missing in this neighborhood."

"That's more likely the Watson's dog," I say. "Grandpa says he's a menace and should be shot."

"Well, if she doesn't eat cats, what does she eat? She never leaves that house, so where does she get her food?"

"She has a garden," I say. "And the delivery boy brings her groceries once a week. He leaves them on the back porch. I've seen him do it."

"And where does she get the money to pay for

those?"

I stop to consider this for a minute. "I don't know. I suppose her husband must have left her some."

"Did he? Or is she making her money some other way?"

I stop Janie with a hand on her arm. "What way?"

"I don't know. Maybe selling information to Hitler. She's German you know."

"So just because she's German, you think she's a spy?"

"Could be. There are spies all over this country. That's why they tell us not to talk about what we make at the factory. You never know who might be listening. I heard they arrested a German man over in LaSalle the other day, less than a mile from Westclox. They confiscated his gun, his typewriter and his camera. They took him and his whole family into custody."

We start to walk again, and I think about Mrs. Osthoff rushing out of that theater, her son's face still fresh on her mind, and I feel a funny urge to defend her. All she's ever wanted is to be left alone, and everyone did just that until the war came along, this war that is changing everything. "She's not a spy," I insist. "My own grandmother is German and no one is accusing her of anything."

"That's different. She doesn't act German, and she was born right here in America. Not like Mrs. Osthoff. They say she doesn't even speak English."

"She speaks a little," I say.

"How do you know? Have you heard her?"

I haven't, of course. The only sounds I've ever heard from Mrs. Osthoff are those horrible screams and those long, low moans. Just thinking of them makes me shudder.

We're approaching Mr. Rodriguez's pool hall. He was a schoolmate of Mother's, and she says he's a good man, that his pool hall is not like most, but not even that sways Grandma Kate. She absolutely forbids me to set foot in any pool hall, even his. "It's no place for a young lady," she says. Janie's mother obviously doesn't agree. Janie's been allowed to hang out there since she was thirteen. Janie knows I can't go in, but she tells me she's going to stop for a minute anyway.

"Maxine got a new pair of saddle shoes and I want to see them quick."

"Come on, Janie. They're just shoes. What's the difference?"

"Oh honestly, Helen. You don't know a thing about fashion."

Janie bounds up the steps into the pool hall, tossing her head as she enters so her blond ponytail swishes attractively. Janie's hair *is* her best feature, high humidity or none, and she uses it to her advantage. I plop down on the second step to pout. I could follow Janie inside, of course. I'm not such a goody two-shoes that I always do what I'm told, but Hayden's Valley is a very small town, and word would get back to Grandma for sure. Mr. Rodriguez himself might tell her, and since Janie will only be in there for a minute, it's not worth the risk.

The clouds are still heavy and low, and I hope it won't rain again. I'm looking at my own worn shoes, wondering if we'll be able to afford a new pair before school starts. Just then I hear some boys come around the building from the left. They stop on the other side of the rhododendron bush that grows at the foot of the steps. I can't see them, but I recognize their voices. One is Hal. The other two are his best friends, Jack and Richie.

"I'll be seventeen on Tuesday," Hal is saying. "That's plenty old to fight."

"Ah, Hal. Your ma'll never let you sign up," Richie says. "You know that."

"Well, she don't have to."

"You can't sign up at seventeen without a parent's permission," Jack says.

"That's why nobody's gonna *know* I'm seventeen. I'm gonna hitch a ride to Peoria. No one will recognize me there."

"But you gotta have proof," Jack says.

"Nah, I got that all figured out. All you need's a Bible to prove your age. You know how people write in their Bibles the dates when their kin are born or die? You just tell the recruiter you lost your birth certificate and show him the family Bible instead."

"But your ma already wrote your correct date in," Richie says.

"Don't be so thick, Rich. I won't take our real Bible. I'll buy myself a new one and fill it in."

"That'll never work," Jack says.

"It sure will. I heard of a guy who did it."

There's silence while the boys consider what Hal's proposing. I realize I've been holding my breath, and I let it out softly. I slip down a step so I can hear better over the rowdy sounds from the pool hall. Jack lets out a long, low whistle.

"Ah, heck, Hal, this is big," Richie says.

"You should come with me," Hal says.

"Nah. My dad would skin me alive, runnin' off like that. I'll be eighteen in six months anyway."

"You should have someone else fill in that Bible," Jack suggests. "So's it don't look like your handwritin'."

"Good idea," Hal says, and just then I realize they are moving. I stand up and try to make it look like I was just coming down the stairs, but Hal knows me too well. His eyes narrow, and he takes me by the wrist and pulls me back around the bush.

"What'd you hear, Lanie?"

"Nothing."

"You're such a bad liar, Helen. Tell me what you heard."

"I heard you telling your friends you're gonna run away and join up. Hal, do you know how stupid that is?"

"It ain't stupid. It's what I want."

"But you could get killed!"

49

"Lots of fellas are gettin' killed while I just sit here. I'm one of the best shots in the Valley. I can take care of myself." He pushes his glasses up, and that reminds me of something.

"Aha! That's why you can't sign up," I tell him. "You're nearly blind without your glasses. You'll never pass the eye exam."

He smirks at me and drops my wrist. "Oh I'll pass all right," he says. "I memorized the eye chart, and I been practicing how to say it so it don't *sound* memorized. Want to hear?"

"No," I say, covering my ears like a baby. I need a second to think, but with my ears covered, I can suddenly hear the whir of bombs dropping in the newsreel footage and the blasts when they hit their targets, and I realize I have to stop Hal from going off to fight.

"I'll tell," I say. "I'll tell your mother. She'll keep such a strict eye on you, you'll never get away."

Hal pushes me up against the wall of the building, both hands on my shoulders. I know he'd never hurt me, but I've never seen him so angry and it scares me.

"You gotta promise not to tell a soul, Helen. Not

even Janie."

"I can't."

"You owe me, Helen. Haven't I always done things for you and never asked nothin' in return? Didn't I fix up that bike for you when you wanted one? Didn't I take the blame when your schoolbooks fell in the river? Wasn't it me who helped you learn your sums? You're a smart girl, Lanie, but you never would have passed those tests without my help."

He's right, of course. Looking at Hal now, with the rain-clear light making his features sharp, I can see on his face he's counting on me. He's never done that before. I feel myself sag against the wall, and he removes his hands from my shoulders, but his voice is still firm.

"Promise," he says. "Promise you won't tell."

I look at my shoes again, but now all I notice is how the edges are growing wet from the grass and how my feet are about the same size as Hal's, and I hear myself say, "Okay. . . I won't tell."

Hal takes a step back and studies me for a minute. He reaches out and rubs my shoulder a bit, like he's worried it might hurt. It doesn't. Nothing hurts except my head, and maybe my heart.

"Thank you, Lanie," he says. "You wait and see. I'll do you proud in the army. Maybe I'll even bring home a medal."

He's smiling now, and he's once again the old Hal, the one who spent a whole summer building me and Janie a tree house. I can't imagine Hayden's Valley without him.

He backs away, then turns and heads over to his buddies, who have watched the whole scene. The three of them glance up at the pool hall, then decide to head back up Main Street instead. Hal looks just once over his shoulder at me, and it's not a friendly, good-bye kind of look, but more like he's making sure I'll keep my promise, and that's when I feel my frustration rise.

It's not fair what he's asking me to do, to just let him go off and get himself shot. It's not fair to ask me to keep such a secret. I've seen the newsreels. I know what happens in war. And Hal's in worse danger than most. What if he loses his glasses? What if they break? Then being the best shot in Hayden's Valley won't help him a bit.

So I make a decision I know will cost me Hal's friendship, but it's better than being responsible for his death. I'll find a way to tell Janie. I won't break my promise to Hal, I won't tell her directly what he plans to do, but there's a guessing game we sometimes play, and if she guesses, then that's different. I pace the sidewalk outside the building for several minutes, but Janie doesn't appear. Finally, I run up the stairs and into the pool hall, but I don't see her anywhere. I take a tentative step inside and call her name. Several kids turn, but none are Janie.

I ask some of the kids gathered around a pool table. One of the older boys cues up a shot. "Janie left," he says. "Went off with Maxine."

I look toward the open back door and realize that's why I didn't see her leave.

"Where'd they go?"

"Don't know."

I rush across the room and look out the back door. I expect to see Janie sitting out back talking to Maxine, but no one's there. And no one is in the alley either. While I was out front trying to save her brother, Janie was leaving me behind to run off with Maxine Land. If it was anybody but Maxine, I might not mind so much. But Maxine's been trying to steal Janie's friendship for months now. She likes the way

Janie dotes on everything she says and does.

I'm so angry I feel tears stinging the backs of my eyes, and I make for home before any of the kids see them fall. When I get there, I head straight to my room. If Janie comes looking for me, I'll tell Mother to send her away. That way she'll know she can't just ditch me whenever the mood strikes.

I'll figure out what to do about Hal tomorrow. He said he wasn't leaving for a few days anyway. There's plenty of time.

5

The Accident

I didn't see Janie at church the next day. Mrs. Brey
said she was ill, but I wasn't sure that was true. I
thought she was avoiding me, feeling bad maybe for
leaving me like that. I considered telling Mrs. Brey
about Hal, but he was watching me carefully, and
I never got the chance. I was planning on telling
Janie today at work, but she didn't show up for the
morning train. I guess maybe she really is sick.

It's hard to concentrate on my job today. I keep
thinking about Hal and how much he's gonna hate
me when I tell his sister what he plans to do, and I
wonder if maybe I should just keep my mouth shut
and let him go. And now I've got my cousin John on
my mind, too. My aunt came over for Sunday dinner
yesterday and sobbed, right there at the table. She

said a transport ship had been sunk on the way to Europe, and what if John was on it? Now I'm worried too and feeling guilty on top of it all. There's a letter to John sitting half-finished on my nightstand. He'd asked me to write, and I'd promised I would, but I've had other things on my mind these last couple of weeks. Silly things, now that I think of them. Like this fight with Janie.

In the midst of all my dark thoughts, I hear a voice. It's Martha.

"I told you to slow down," she says, "not let them pass altogether."

"Huh?"

She waves in the direction of the conveyor belt, and I see that I've let a piece pass me right by. Betty has pulled it off the line and set it next to her drill, grinning at me smugly.

"I guess I wasn't paying attention," I say, reaching for the next piece.

"Got your mind on bigger things?" Betty asks.

"Some fella, no doubt." Martha adds.

I'm in no mood for their teasing. The rain clouds that favored us over the weekend have lifted, and it's hotter than ever in the assembly room today. I didn't have time to fix my hair this morning, and it's so frizzy I can't keep it out of my eyes. I brush it away with the back of my hand.

"Poor little Helen," Martha says. "So young to have boy troubles already."

Betty laughs. It's a laugh that's a little too loud and a little too deep to be real.

I lean closer to my drill, trying to shut out the sights and sounds of these women, but Martha keeps right on going.

"Why, when I was her age, Betty, I wouldn't have dared even talk to a boy. But girls are a bit fresher nowadays, don't you think? What with the war and all."

I move still closer to my drill.

"Oops, you missed another one," Martha says.

I'm sure it's not true, but I turn my head to the left to check the belt just in case, and that's when my hair gets caught in the spinning drill bit. I feel my head jerk forward and start banging against the drill press. *Thump, thump, thump.* My head is aching, and my scalp is burning where the hair is being torn loose. I hear someone scream. It sounds like Rita.

"Turn it off, Helen!" she's shouting.

Someone else is calling for Mr. Mueller, the foreman. I reach around to the back of the drill press and turn it off. As the bit stops turning, I manage to untangle myself. There's a quarter-size clump of hair that's been ripped from my head, and when I touch my fingertips to my scalp, they come away bloody. My headache is getting worse now, and I feel faint from the heat, but mostly I'm embarrassed as several women gather around. I can't believe I let Martha and Betty get to me. I want to prove to everyone that I can take care of myself, so I push Rita's helpful hands away. I accept a handkerchief from one woman, though, and hold it to my head. Just then, Mr. Mueller appears, his thick moustache quivering above his twitching lip.

"What happened here?" he demands.

"Helen got her hair caught."

"Well, I can see that. Where was your hair net, girl?"

I stare at him, feeling like I need to sit down. "What net, sir?"

He fixes his hands on his hips and rises on his toes so he can look me in the eye. "The one I told you to wear on your first day here."

"You never told her nothin'," Martha says. "You wasn't here."

He glares at Martha, and I can tell he doesn't like her any more than the rest of us do, but this time she's telling the truth.

"That's right," Rita agrees. "I think you were out that day, Mr. Mueller."

He looks from woman to woman and they all confirm Rita's words with slight nods of their heads.

"Humph," he says, dropping back onto his heels. "All right, then. Rita will take you down to see the doc. Then you go on home, girl."

"I don't need to go home, sir. I'll be fine." If I clock out early, I won't get my full day's pay.

He puffs out his chest. "I'm the foreman here, and I say you go home. I don't want some slow-handed girl whining about her aching head all day."

"More like you don't want your supervisor finding out you blew the record," Betty says, with a nod toward the company sign for our department that boasts: 63 Days Without an Accident.

"Just get her out of here," Mr. Mueller says. "And wear your hair net from now on, girl."

I want to scream at him to stop calling me girl,

59

but I don't. He's still my boss, though he's not much of one, and I don't want to get myself fired. I let Rita lead me down to the medical center, and the nurse takes a look at my head. She slows the bleeding and gives me some aspirin for the pain, then shows me how to comb my hair over the bald spot. She too reminds me to wear a hair net, and I say I will, but I won't. None of the women do. I'll just be more careful from now on.

I wait for an hour in the heat for a bus to take me back to Hayden's Valley, my head throbbing. When I get home, Grandma Kate settles me on the front porch, where the scent of the neighbor's freshly cut grass greets me on a breeze. She brings me a glass of lemonade and a Nancy Drew mystery, but I don't feel like reading. I feel like crying. I had been so excited for this summer, for having my own job and being with Janie, and now between the war and Hal and Mother's injury and Martha and Betty, nothing about this summer is working out as I'd planned. I go ahead and let a few tears fall, but things are about to get worse.

6

The Telegram

When the Western Union boy turns up our walkway, telegram in hand, I jump up, my heart racing. I can tell by the grim look on his face that his news isn't good.

There's not a family in town who doesn't dread a visit like this, one that brings news of a soldier's death or injury. We've all heard the story about the father in LaSalle who received a telegram telling him both of his sons had died when the Japanese attacked Pearl Harbor. All I can think of now is John. But why would the Western Union man be bringing the telegram here and not to my aunt's house?

"Grandma!" I yell, and I must sound pretty scared, because she rushes out on the porch almost immediately.

The telegram boy shuffles his feet. I recognize him now. He's Mr. Anderson's oldest son. "Sorry to bother you, Mrs. Uhland," he says. "I been trying to deliver this telegram to the house behind you. I know someone's home cuz the front door is open, but no one answers when I ring. The neighbor said I ought to bring it here and give it to you."

Grandma Kate extends a hand. "I'll sign for it and see that Mrs. Osthoff gets it."

"Thank you, ma'am."

The boy hands the telegram to Grandma Kate and ambles back down the walkway, his footsteps lightened by the release of his sad duty. Grandma and I stare at the star on the cover of the telegram, then she turns it over and slips it open. Over her shoulder, I read the words in capital letters: THE SECRETARY OF WAR DESIRES TO EXPRESS HIS DEEP REGRET YOUR SON PRIVATE FREDERICK OSTHOFF WAS KILLED IN ACTION. . . I don't see the rest. Grandma Kate has dropped down onto the porch swing, letting the telegram fall into her lap.

"Merciful heavens," she says. "Hasn't that poor woman been through enough?"

She sinks back against the swing, and I sit down

beside her. She lays a hand on my knee, and I lower my head to her shoulder. I rock the swing with my foot, the chains creaking beneath our shared weight. Neither of us says a word until Grandma sighs heavily and shakes me off.

"Tell your mother I'll be back soon," she says, her voice strong and clear again.

"Can I come with you?"

"No."

"Please, Grandma. I just want to tell her I'm sorry for her loss." This isn't entirely true, I'm ashamed to admit. I also want to see Mrs. Osthoff up close. Maybe catch a glimpse into that closed-up house of hers. And I want to see how Grandma Kate handles this situation, she who can handle anything. But how do you tell someone her son is gone? I have to see that for myself. I'm sure Grandma knows I have other motives—she always knows exactly what I'm thinking—but she surprises me by saying yes. I guess this is something she doesn't want to do alone. I slip my shoes on quickly before she changes her mind.

Grandma Kate would never dream of cutting through people's lawns, so we walk all the way around the block to reach Mrs. Osthoff's house. Grandma pauses for only a moment to draw a deep breath, then plows up the porch steps and knocks on the screen door. The inside door is open.

"Eva," she calls, and I'm surprised to hear her use Mrs. Osthoff's first name.

"Eva, come to the door." When there is still no movement in the house, Grandma Kate opens the screen door and lets herself in. I follow.

There is no entryway in this house. We've stepped directly into Mrs. Osthoff's sitting room. It's not at all what I expected. With all the rumors about her, I imagined dark, dusty rooms littered with broken and discarded things. But this room is not like that at all. It's as neat and tidy as our own. The furniture is old but well cared for, and the walls are decorated with framed photographs and embroidered samplers that look recently completed. The house smells of rose blossoms from a vase near the window. The curtains are drawn, but there is light coming in from the front door.

"Eva," Grandma Kate calls out again, then takes herself down the hall to the kitchen.

Mrs. Osthoff is sitting at her kitchen table,

her hand resting on her chin, her eyes gazing out through the lace curtains toward the back of our house. She looks thin in her old brown house dress. Her ankles are crossed above dark, heavy shoes, and there's a small hole in her hose. Her hair is pulled back in a loose bun. In the light from the window, though, I can see it's still a pretty shade of auburn with only traces of grey. Grandma lays a hand on Mrs. Osthoff's shoulder and sets the telegram gently in front of her. Mrs. Osthoff looks down at it. There are deep shadows under her eyes, and her cheeks are pale, but she is not unattractive, and she does not look crazy. She just looks sad.

I hold onto the doorway, afraid to move closer, afraid Mrs. Osthoff will release one of her terrible screams, but she doesn't. She just hugs herself and starts to shake. Grandma puts her arm around Mrs. Osthoff and does something so unexpected it steals my breath. She starts speaking to Mrs. Osthoff—*in German*. She does this for several minutes, stroking the younger woman's hair. Then Mrs. Osthoff does scream, "Frederick!" She throws off Grandma's arm and brushes past me, slamming her bedroom door. I hear that long, low moan I know so well, and it's worse than the scream because it's filled with so much pain. I shudder. Grandma Kate straightens and looks past me for a moment, then lets her shoulders drop. There are tears in her eyes. In all my fourteen years, I've never seen my grandmother cry. I start to say something, but she just turns me around and pushes me ahead of her out the front door.

Outside, she starts walking so fast that even my long legs can barely keep up.

"Grandma?" I say, but she shushes me.

She storms through our front door and back to the kitchen without even taking off her shoes. She grabs an apron off the peg and reaches under the sink for her boiling pot, banging it down on the stove. She picks up a potato off the counter and starts to whip the peel off with quick, hard strokes. I know I should help, but I sink down into a chair and watch instead.

"Grandma, you called Mrs. Osthoff by her first name," I say. "It sounded like you knew her."

"Well, of course I do. Haven't I lived across from that woman for years?"

"No, it sounded like more than that. Like you *really* knew her. And you were speaking German,

Grandma. I didn't know you knew how."

She drops her knife into the sink and turns on me. "Of course I know how. Weren't my parents from Germany? Didn't they move here just before I was born? Half the folks in this valley have German blood, Helen. That doesn't make us Nazis."

"Of course not," I say, but that's exactly what I'd been thinking, and Grandma knew it. I wonder if the police will come search our home too, like they did that German man's in LaSalle. Grandma picks up her knife and starts chopping the potato. I shouldn't say any more, but I can't help it.

"Is that why you're friends with Mrs.Osthoff? Cuz she's German too?"

"I am not *friends* with Mrs. Osthoff. Her husband, Otto, was a distant relative of mine from Germany. Otto wrote to us after the First World War. He had married a young woman whose heart was broken. She'd lost everything. He thought a fresh start in a new country would do her good." Grandma picks up another potato that's already peeled and starts chopping that one too. "We helped them get settled when they got here. At first they lived in an apartment above the pool hall, then they moved into the house behind us. Frederick was born there." She scoops up the potatoes and dumps them into the pot.

"After Frederick's birth," she says, "Eva started talking again. She took up photography. She got good at it too. She was happy . . . for a while. After Otto died, she closed herself up in that house with her son, but Frederick was never meant for a life like that. He was a dreamer. He wanted to see the world. He couldn't stay there with her and her grief. After Frederick left, Eva shut us out. All of us. Even me."

Grandma Kate pauses. She slumps over the sink. For a moment I think she might be crying again, but when she looks up her eyes are clear and hard.

"Grandma?"

"Enough of your questions, Helen. Go check on your mother. Let me have some peace."

I take off my shoes and slip into the back bedroom. When the heat is high in the daytime, we all rest in this room. It's too hot upstairs. Mother is sleeping, so I decide not to wake her. I go back out to the front porch and arrange the pillows so I can curl up on the porch swing and wait for Grandpa George. I close my eyes and concentrate on what has just happened. Every time I think I know all there is to know about this family, I find out something else, like the fact that my grandmother speaks German and that our crazy neighbor is practically a member of our family. Grown-ups scold children for keeping secrets, but it seems to me they have plenty of secrets themselves.

I'd almost forgotten about my head in the excitement of the afternoon. Now I touch it gingerly. It's still sore. I sit up to look down the street for Grandpa. "What did I miss?" he always asks when he returns from an errand. It's his way of being funny, because nothing much of interest ever happens around our house.

But today I'll have plenty to tell him.

7

My Mistake

Before light the next morning, I'm eating breakfast at the kitchen table when someone bangs on the back door. I turn on the porch light. It's Janie. If she's here to apologize, I'm not going to make it easy for her. I cross my arms and look at her coolly, but then I notice that her face is flushed, and my heart sinks.

"What is it, Janie?" Grandma asks, coming up beside me and lifting the screen door latch to let her in.

"Oh Mrs. Uhland. Hal ran off last night. He left a note saying he was going to join up. Daddy wants to know if he can borrow your car. He wants to drive to LaSalle and see if Hal's at the recruiting station there."

"He's not," I hear myself whisper.

"What's that, Helen?" Grandma says.

I clear my throat. "He's not in LaSalle. He's in Peoria."

"Merciful heavens. Did you know about this, child?"

Janie stares at me.

"I didn't think he'd leave so soon," I blurt out. "It's only just his birthday."

"You knew?" Janie's scowling at me. "You knew and you didn't tell me?"

"I couldn't! You were off with Maxine Land."

"I was only gone a minute. If you'd been patient for once in your life, you'd have known that."

"Oh Helen," Grandma Kate says, as if I don't feel bad enough. "Wait here, Janie. I'll fetch the car keys."

"I'll go back with you," I tell Janie. "We can leave for work from your house after I talk to your parents."

"I'm not going to work today. I'm going to help look for my brother."

"But you missed yesterday. You'll get fired."

"I didn't miss. I got a ride there and back with my neighbor. She was spending the day in LaSalle and I didn't want to ride the train."

"You mean you didn't want to ride with *me*."

"Okay, yes. That was part of it. One of the boys told me you stormed off Saturday night. I thought it was ridiculous for you to be so mad. But I never would have imagined you'd keep something like *this* from me just to get even."

"I didn't keep it from you, Janie. I meant to tell you about Hal. Then yesterday things just . . . happened. My hair and Frederick and Mrs. Osthoff. I just forgot. Honest."

Just then, Grandma Kate reappears with the keys.

Janie thanks her and turns to go. I call to her, but she doesn't look back at me.

"Come and finish your breakfast," Grandma Kate says. "You'll miss your train."

"I'm not going to work."

"Nonsense. There's nothing you can do here. Mr. Brey will find Hal or he won't. That's just the way of things."

But it didn't have to have been the way of things, I realize, not if I'd done what I should have. If I'm so grown up, why do I keep making such childish mistakes? But I did tell them Hal went to Peoria. Maybe that will be enough. Surely Mr. Brey will find him there and bring him home. Then I can make things up with Janie.

I haven't touched my eggs and toast since Janie showed up, and now Grandma whisks my plate away, pushing me roughly out of my chair. "Go to work," she says. "You'll feel better when you get there."

I don't believe her at first, but as I trudge toward the train depot alone, I think maybe work is the best place for me. At least there I do things right. And if I can't save Hal from leaving, I can at least help bring him home quicker by working hard, by making timing devices for those bombs that will sail right over those German cities. I can help make sure that nobody else's son has to die like Mrs. Osthoff's and that no one thinks twice about *our* family's loyalty, despite our German blood. And when my paycheck comes this Friday, I'm gonna ask Mother if we can spare a few cents to buy war stamps, like the Westclox supervisors encourage us to do. One ten-cent stamp would pay for five bullets. A twenty-five-cent stamp could buy a soldier's mess kit. So little can do so much.

I can make up for my mistake with Hal if I work hard enough, and if Martha or Betty try to get in my way, I'll find a way to deal with them once and for all.

8

The Garden

When I get home from work that evening, there is still no word from Janie. Mother telephones Mrs. Brey and finds out Mr. Brey called from Peoria. Hal had never been there. He must have guessed I'd tell them and gone somewhere else. Springfield, maybe, or even Chicago. Mr. Brey and Janie are on their way home. They'll drop the car off soon. Grandma Kate must have been in no mood to cook, so fried cornmeal is all we get and that's fine by me. I'm not hungry anyway, and I want to make sure I'm finished and up in my room when Janie and her father arrive. I can't face either of them yet.

"This is not your fault," Mother says to me.

"Hal's practically a grown man," Grandpa George adds. "If his mind was made up, nothing was going to stop him."

"But they might have talked him out of it," I say. "Mr. Brey might have convinced him he's needed at the store."

"That's not how a young man's mind works, Helen. When I was Hal's age, I wanted to join in fighting the Spanish down in Cuba. But my father was dead, and my mother couldn't manage the farm on her own. If it hadn't been for that, I just might have run off to war myself."

I can't picture my grandfather in a soldier's uniform. He doesn't even like guns and has no heart for killing. He hates shooting even a squirrel or a duck for our dinner. I know he's trying to make me feel better, but I'd rather change the subject.

"Did you see Mrs. Osthoff today?"

Mother and Grandma Kate exchange a look across the table. "That poor woman wants to be left alone, Helen," Grandma says.

"But I do worry, Mama," Mother adds. "I worry she'll stop taking care of herself."

"Give it a few days," Grandpa George says. "Then we'll check on her again."

I skip dessert. It's just peaches anyway. We're out

of cream. I hide out in our room, trying to finish my letter to John. But when I hear our car pull up to the driveway behind our house, I go to the window. I hear Mr. Brey talking to Grandpa, apologizing for the wear he put on our tires. With rubber in such high demand, there will be no new tires until after the war. Grandpa tells him not to worry, that he can take the car out again tomorrow if he wants, but Mr. Brey says no. He figures they'll just wait to hear from Hal. If they fetched him home now, he might just run off again anyway. I risk a peek out the window and see Janie still sitting in our car. She's hiding, just like me.

After they leave, I pick up my Nancy Drew book, *Mystery of the Moss-Covered Mansion*. It came out last year, and I've read it through once already, but I always read Nancy Drews at least twice. Janie says I'm too old for these books, but I like the way Nancy knows how to handle any situation. Grandpa George would say she has "pluck." I used to think I had that too. As the evening wears on, I hear the crickets chirping outside my window and a dog barking down the street. The sounds of kids playing are starting to fade as they get called inside for bed. Mother knocks on my door and pokes her head in to check on me. I don't turn over to look at her, just mumble goodnight, and she gently closes the door.

When it's grown late enough that I would need a light to keep reading, I close the book and go to my window to let the twilight settle in around me. I rest my head against the windowpane and watch Grandma Kate putting away her garden tools. She sets the watering can next to the shed and heads back to the house. The lightning bugs flicker across the yard. From the open window below come muffled voices from the radio. Grandpa's listening to war news, which makes me think of John. If something had happened to him, I'd feel it, right? He's my favorite cousin, after all. And once when we were little, one of the kids came running up to a teacher and said a boy had fallen out of the tree. I knew immediately it was John, and I've always wondered how I knew. Since I don't feel anything now, he must be all right, over there in the Pacific somewhere. I wonder if he flies at night, like they do in the movies, right into the sunset. I wonder if he'll bring me back a souvenir from the war. I try not to wonder about Hal and where he'll wind up or whether I'll feel it if something happens to him too.

Just then, there's a movement in Mrs. Osthoff's yard, and my heart quickens. I imagine it's her, coming out to check her garden. That's what I hope, anyway. I didn't see her last night, and I've got Mother's words echoing in my ears: "I worry she'll stop taking care of herself." I lean forward for a better look, but it's just an old tomcat prowling around her lawn, and I remember what Janie said about Mrs. Osthoff eating cats. Now that I've seen her, I know it's not true, and I wish people would leave her alone. I imagine her sitting over there missing her son, and I feel a little ashamed for thinking my own problems are so big. There's no light from her kitchen window. She won't be checking on her garden tonight either. In this heat, it will wilt quickly if no one tends it. She has little enough to eat as it is. I make up my mind what I should do.

Grandma has made it clear I should leave Mrs. Osthoff alone, but sometimes you gotta help people even when they don't think they want you to. Maybe that's why Hal told his friends his plan. Maybe he *wanted* someone to stop him, and I just didn't act fast enough. I wait until the radio goes silent and I hear Grandma and Grandpa close their bedroom door, and then I wait fifteen minutes more until I hear Grandpa's snores on the other side of my wall. Then I sneak down the stairs and out the back. I grab the watering can and fill it at the back sink, hoping no one will come down to check when they hear the water running. But no one does, so I push open our back gate, cross the alley and step over the foot-high wall that edges Mrs. Osthoff's property.

In the light of the moon, I water that little garden, squatting down to pick out a weed or two from around the carrots and beets and small cabbage heads. When I'm finished, I hurry back to my own yard, careful to put the can back exactly as I found it. I get that old feeling that I'm being watched, but when I look back toward Mrs. Osthoff's windows, I see nothing. The garden will need more than one can of water, I realize. Tomorrow evening I'll use the hose to fill the can and a pail or two before everyone goes to bed, so I don't have to risk the noise again.

I'm feeling better now. Grandpa once told me that growing up doesn't mean we stop making mistakes, it means we start making up for the mistakes we make.

9

The Spy

The following Saturday afternoon, I return from
running an errand for Grandma to find all thirteen
members of the Hayden's Valley Women's Club
perched in chairs in my backyard. They look very
summery in their lightweight cotton dresses in floral
prints, fanning themselves and drinking lemonade
from tall glasses. Mother nods me over, and I drop
down on the grass at her feet.

"Did you return the books to the library?"
Grandma asks.

"Yep. Oh and they're doing a rubber drive at the
filling station, Grandma," I say. "They're collecting
all kinds of things. Garden hoses, baby dolls, even
girdles."

"Oh my," Mrs. Anderson says. "Well, they can

certainly have mine if they want it."

As the rest of the women joke about what other undergarments they'd love to get rid of, Mother leans down and asks me, "Did you see Janie in town?"

"No. I went by her house, but she wasn't home. Mrs. Brey says they've had a telegram from Hal, though. He's headed to basic training, but he didn't say where. I guess he's still afraid they'll try to find him. I told Mrs. Brey again how sorry I am, and she said it wasn't my fault. I guess Janie still thinks it is though. I'm sure that's why she quit her job at Westclox."

"She'll come around," Mother says. "Friends always do."

I rest my arms lightly across Mother's lap and lean my chin on my arms. If her hands were free, she'd rub my back as she's done since I was a little girl, when we used to sit like this and listen to *Little Orphan Annie* on the radio.

"How's your job, Helen?" Mrs. Anderson says, and I raise my head.

"It's fine," I say, and it is right now, except that Janie's gone. But Martha left on Wednesday to visit her mother in Chicago and won't be back for a week.

Without her at work, Betty seems to have lost her courage for stirring up trouble. Rita is back from her quick honeymoon, and she's smiling again, and the line is moving along nicely.

"Well, your mother tells us you've been working awfully hard this summer," Mrs. Anderson continues. "She's quite proud of you."

"Yes, we're all proud of her," Grandma interrupts. "Now if she'd only put as much effort into her chores at home. Was there something I asked you to do before you left, Helen?"

I blush as I remember the wash I was supposed to hang on the line.

"Sorry, Grandma," I say, sitting up.

"Oh don't be too hard on her, Kate. This is an exciting time for young girls," Mrs. Land says. "My own Maxine went to a dance in Streator the other day with her cousin and met a soldier there. Said she danced with him all night. She was wearing her navy blue jacket dress, the one with the organdy trim. That dress would look quite fetching on you, Helen. I'm sure Maxine would let you borrow it sometime, but of course you're too tall for it."

I start to slouch, just like I always do when

someone mentions my height, but Mother nudges me with her knee, and I straighten back up. Then, thankfully, Mother changes the subject.

"We're meeting here to decide on a service project, Helen. We're going to knit socks and mufflers for the soldiers. Grandma says she'll teach you how to knit if you want to help."

Before I can answer, a high, piercing scream splits the air. The fans stop in the women's hands, and all eyes turn to Mrs. Osthoff's house.

"That woman," Mrs. Fuller says. "Will she never let up?"

"She lost her son," Mother says quietly. "I expect that gives her reason to be upset."

"Now, Barbara, she carried on like that before Frederick died. You know that. If you ask me, she's pining away for her homeland, wishing she could go back."

"Then you think it's true what they say?" Mrs. Land asks. "You think she's some sort of German spy?"

"Well, I don't know. But take a look at that weather vane atop the house. Do you see that it's stuck? My Stanley pointed that out. And it's facing *north*, right toward the center of town. Could be a signal, don't you think? For the Nazi bombers?"

"That's ridiculous," I hear myself say. The women all turn to look at me with surprise, so I rush to explain. "Grandpa says the German planes won't come this far inland and, besides, a pilot would need something bigger than a weather vane for a signal. He'd never see something that small from a cockpit. Everyone knows that."

"Helen," Grandma cautions. "Careful of your tone."

"I'm sorry, Grandma, but it's true. If John were here, he'd tell you." I glare at Mrs. Land. "Mrs. Osthoff is not a spy."

"Well, there's something strange about that woman," Mrs. Land says. "It's just not normal keeping oneself shut up like that. Especially not in times like these."

"You're absolutely right," Mrs. Fuller says. "Here we sit, after all, proving *our* devotion to the war effort, and she's the one who has something to prove."

"Did you invite her to join you?" I ask. "Maybe she would have wanted to knit socks for the soldiers.

You didn't even give her a chance."

"Helen," Grandma Kate says. "That's quite enough."

"Well, it isn't fair," I mumble. "Mrs. Osthoff isn't bothering anyone. Why can't people just leave her alone?"

Mrs. Fuller cocks her head and studies me. "Well, I didn't realize you were so fond of the elusive Mrs. Osthoff, Helen. Why is that?"

I think back on how Mrs. Osthoff looked when Grandma Kate told her the news about Frederick, how even sitting there with Grandma's arm around her shoulder she looked so totally alone. It seemed so unfair for one person to suffer so much.

"I just feel sorry for her, that's all," I answer back.

"I think we all do," Mrs. Anderson says, smiling at me gently.

"Yes, of course," Mrs. Land continues, taking a sip of her lemonade. "But that weather vane is most certainly stuck."

All eyes return to Mrs. Osthoff's house, and it's not until Grandma Kate brings up yarn color for the mufflers that the conversation turns back to the war effort. Grandma hands me the knitting patterns she'd brought out and sends me inside to put them away.

"Bunch of old biddies," I say to myself as I cross the living room toward Grandma's favorite chair. As I reach for her knitting sack, I realize I'm mad at her too. She could have stood up for Mrs. Osthoff. She knows her better than any of us. But she didn't. She just sat there rubbing her eyes.

Grandpa George stirs. I hadn't noticed him dozing in his chair, the morning newspaper spread across his lap. He sits upright, rubbing his neck.

"Did I wake you?" I ask.

"That's all right," he says, readjusting his glasses. "I'm just going to finish this paper, then get myself a snack." He picks up the newspaper and starts to read. I lean across the settee and look out the front window up and down the street. I don't see any of the neighbor kids. I plop down on the settee, bored, and watch Grandpa read.

"How's it going?" I ask. "I mean the war."

Grandpa glances at me over the paper. "I didn't think you were interested."

"I wasn't," I admit. "I kind of hoped it would all just go away, but that's not going to happen, is it?"

"No, it's not, honey. Things are not going in the

Allies' favor. We've got a long, hard fight ahead of us."

I go and sit on the arm of his chair as he folds up his newspaper. "Where will John be stationed?"

"Don't know yet. We set up a code so he can tell us when he gets there."

"How will it work?"

"He's going to spell out the name of the base where he's stationed. Each time he sends a letter to your aunt, he'll use a different middle initial, and eventually the initials will spell out the base."

"Then he'll have to write quite a few letters at first."

"Yes, well that may be the problem with our plan. I don't think John is much of a letter writer."

"If he gets stationed in Britain, he'll be fighting only the Nazis, right?"

"Yes."

"And the Japanese are only in the Pacific?"

"Yes, but that's a pretty big place. Here, I have an idea," he says, pushing himself out of his chair. He crosses into the dining room and I follow. He opens the top drawer of the buffet and removes a battered map of the world and spreads it across the table. He points out the places where American forces are fighting.

I study the map for a minute in silence. "Where do you think Hal will wind up?"

"Hard to say. He could wind up in Britain, but more likely they'll send him to the Pacific to fight the Japs."

"And where did Frederick die?"

Grandpa's finger hovers above the map for a moment, before he sets it slowly down. "Here, in the Coral Sea in the South Pacific."

"So far away."

"Yes." We both stare at Grandpa's finger and the far-off spot where it points on the map.

"It's such a big war. It's hard to keep it all straight," I sigh.

"Maybe this will help." Grandpa goes into the kitchen and comes back with a box of pins. He directs me around the corner to the hallway leading to the back bedroom. "Help me put this up," he says, and begins pinning the map to the wall. "We'll use these pins with the colored heads to keep track of our advances in the war in Europe and the Pacific. Then you can see where our troops are moving."

I shake my head, grinning. "Boy is Grandma

gonna be mad when she sees these holes in the wall."

"You let me worry about that," he says, and he does look a bit worried. "Speaking of your grandmother," he says. "I want you to help me glue something. My arthritis is acting up today, and I just can't get my fingers to work."

He pulls out a set of empty seed packets, and I help him glue them on to short stakes. These will serve as markers for everything Grandma grows in the garden, and they make each row look so festive. When we're finished, Grandpa lays a hand on my head. "Why don't you run out now and have some fun."

I consider trying to find Janie, but what if she's with Maxine and still doesn't want to talk to me? I don't want to be embarrassed in front of Maxine. I could head down to the lake. I'm sure to find some kids my age down there, but Janie might be there too. The more I think about Janie, the more I feel sorry for myself. Grandma always says the best way to stop thinking about yourself is to start thinking about someone else. So that's what I do. I think about Mrs. Osthoff and her garden. I don't have Grandma Kate's green thumb, but I've been paying more attention when I help in our own garden, trying to learn as much as I can. If I can keep Mrs. Osthoff's garden alive, maybe one of these days she will take an interest in it again. Then I'll know she'll be all right.

And then it hits me: the one thing missing from Mrs. Osthoff's garden. Those tidy little markers that show where each thing grows. If I work on them this afternoon, I can set them up tonight. We've already used all of Grandma's seed packets, but there are still some leftover stakes. I can write the names of each fruit or vegetable right on the stakes. I can use some black paint Grandpa has in the garage, so the letters won't run in the rain. The markers won't be as showy as Grandma's seed packet ones, but they will give some order to the garden. And she can use them again next year. I'm sure she'll like that.

10

The Photograph

I'm humming when I sneak over to Mrs. Osthoff's
that evening, the little stakes sticking out of my
shorts' pockets. I push the stakes into the soft dirt
and sit back on my heels to admire them, all lined
up in a row. As I tip the watering can over the plants,
I get that prickly feeling again, like someone is
watching me. I look up into the window, and there's
a face behind the lace curtains. It scares me so badly,
I drop the can. Mrs. Osthoff gestures me in.

I glance back at my house, wondering if I should
just run, but that's silly, isn't it? She's my neighbor,
not a ghost. I'm acting like a child. I pick up the
watering can and cradle it in my arms, my heart
beating hard in my chest. As I step into her dark
kitchen, I see Mrs. Osthoff sitting at her table, a red

ripe tomato in front of her.

She's wearing the same brown house dress she wore the last time I saw her, but her feet are bare and her hair is down, brushed smooth and shiny. She gestures to the seat opposite her, and I hesitate before setting the watering can down and pulling out the chair. We sit in silence for a moment. I'm looking at my hands, rubbing at the dirt on my fingertips, but I can feel her eyes on me.

Finally, she clears her throat and I look up. She covers the tomato gently with her hand. "You do this?" she asks.

"Yes. I thought you needed something to eat."

She smiles. "Is good."

"Thank you. There's lots more coming. Tomatoes are easy to grow."

She nods, then raises her hand to tell me to wait and slides her chair back. She crosses the room to the light switch, her hand hesitating for a moment before she turns it on. The room comes to light, and it's not as well-kept as I remember. There are dishes piled by the sink, although neatly, and empty milk bottles lined up on the counter. Cupboard doors stand open, as if she'd lacked the energy even to close them. And there is a smell of something spoiled coming from the pantry. Mrs. Osthoff holds up a glass. "Water?" she asks.

"No, thank you," I say, but she fills the glass anyway and sets it in front of me, slipping back into her chair, her hands folded. She watches me, and I take a sip to be polite. She begins to knead her hands, looking nervous. I realize she is waiting for me to speak next. It's probably been years since she entertained anyone. I want to stay, since she asked me in, but she's looking at me so intently I have to look away. I notice a table in the hallway just outside the kitchen that is covered with framed photographs, and I ask if I can take a look. She nods.

"Who's this?" I hold up a picture of a man with a square jaw and friendly eyes.

She lays a hand across her heart.

"Your husband?" I ask. "Otto?"

She nods, and I point to the picture sitting next to it. It's of a young man in a marine uniform. "Is this Frederick?" She comes to stand beside me, taking the picture gently into her hands and smiling that soft, sad smile.

"I remember him," I say. "He was very nice."

She sets the picture down carefully and picks up a family portrait. There are two parents and five children, dressed all in black, looking straight into the camera. "My family," she says, naming each of them in turn. Then she takes my arm and guides me to a larger photograph hanging on the wall. It's a picture of a farmhouse set amongst rolling hills. To the side of the house, a farmer holds the reins of two large horses. "My home," she says. "Germany."

"It's very pretty," I say. "Is that your father?"

She nods, then her eyebrows knit together, and she turns away. She stands there, staring off at the corner of the room, like she's forgotten I'm there. I wait for a minute, then that prickly feeling returns and I feel like I need to leave. I take a step backward, but the movement brings her back from her thoughts. She stares at me for a moment, like she's not sure who I am. Then her eyes clear, and she takes my arm again and leads me back into the kitchen. I sit back down and wrap my hands around my water glass. "Grandma says you were a good photographer. She says you were always taking pictures."

Mrs. Osthoff nods. Then she jumps up. She raises her hand quickly to tell me to wait and disappears into another room. I hear a drawer open and a shuffling sound, and I glance out the window toward my house. The windows are dark. No one knows I'm here.

When she comes back, she's holding another photograph, this one smaller, with a black border around the edges. She sets it down on the table in front of me. "For you," she says. I pick it up. There are two men in the photograph. One is standing, the other sitting. The one who's sitting is holding a baby in his lap. I recognize the one with the friendly eyes.

"This is Otto," I say.

She nods. Then she points to the baby and taps my chest. It takes me a minute to realize what she's saying.

"Is this me?" I ask, and she nods. She points to the man holding me and says, "Your Papa."

I feel my breath leave in a rush. I've seen portraits of my father before. They decorate my mother's dresser. But I've never seen a picture of him with *me*, and I can't take my eyes off his lean, handsome face. "I don't remember him very well," I explain. "He died when I was three."

"Look his hands," she says. "How gently he holds

95

you."

"I don't remember him holding me," I say. "He had tuberculosis, which is contagious, so he couldn't be near Mother or me."

Mrs. Osthoff motions for me to continue, and I think back to the only memory I have of my father and start to speak it out loud. "We lived in a different town then, near my father's family. My uncles built a garage behind our house. It was a tiny building with only a cot and a chair and a stove inside. My uncles put up screens in the summer, and they built a railing below the window so I could stand on it and see in. My father would talk to me from his bed. Sometimes he'd play his violin."

Mrs. Osthoff motions to me again to go on, but I can't. "That's all I remember," I explain. "I don't even remember when he died."

Mrs. Osthoff nods her understanding, and I feel a strange pull on my heart. Stirring up these memories has made me miss my father more than I ever have before, and for the first time I understand what it is I've really lost. Seeing the pride in my father's eyes in the picture, the way he looks at me so lovingly, I wonder if he would be proud of me still.

And then I realize that if I can miss a father I barely knew, how much harder it must be for Mrs. Osthoff, who lost her parents and siblings in the First World War and then her husband and now her only son. No wonder she screams, I think. No wonder she locks herself up in this house. How can she not think about all the people she's lost, those people in her photographs? How can she not spend all her time missing them? And how can that not make her crazy?

Her eyes have taken on that faraway look. She's remembering too. She turns to stare out the kitchen window.

"Thank you for the picture," I say, but she doesn't answer. Once again, it's as if I'm not even there. I pick up the watering can, but she doesn't seem to notice. I open the back door and turn to look at her once more and then ease the door closed. As I walk across her lawn, I hear that long, low moan. It doesn't scare me this time, though. I understand it now.

I change into my pajamas and crawl into bed, the picture still in my hand. I study it in the moonlight, trying to remember every story my mother has told me about my dad. About how he taught high school

before he took sick and how he and Mother had
hoped to have lots of children and how he used to
play his violin at the church dances. I fall asleep that
night still holding that picture and feeling grateful
to Mrs. Osthoff for the gift she gave me—the gift of
seeing my father and me together—and I vow to find
a way to thank her.

11

Finding My Voice

I look for Mrs. Osthoff Sunday night. She doesn't invite me in, but she smiles at me from her window and offers a shy wave. I leave a tomato and some string beans on her top step and hurry home feeling warm inside. The next morning I rise early for work. Mother and Grandma are already at the kitchen table when I stumble in. "That was quite a commotion last night," Mother is saying.

"What commotion?" I ask.

"Some boys threw a rock through Mrs. Osthoff's kitchen window. I'm surprised you didn't hear it."

My heart sinks. "Is she all right?" I ask, rushing for the back door.

"Come back here and eat your breakfast," Grandma says. "You'll be late for work."

"But I need to check on her," I say, sliding reluctantly into my chair.

"Your grandfather did that last night."

"Did he?"

"Yes. He knocked several times, and there was no answer."

"Then I should go. She'll answer for me."

"Why? Because you've been looking after her garden?"

I glance at Mother. She's looking at me over her cup. I should have guessed they would know.

"It would have been a lot easier to take the hose over rather than lugging that watering can and pail. If you hadn't felt the need to sneak around, you could have done that," Grandma snaps.

"I didn't think you'd let me go," I explain. "You're always saying to leave her alone. Someone had to do something for her."

"Hmm," is all Grandma Kate can say.

"She asked me in on Saturday night, Mother. We talked. She gave me this." I take the picture out of my skirt pocket and hold it up for Mother to see.

"I remember this," Mother says. "This was our first visit home with you, Helen. Look, Mama. Look how well Calvin looks."

Grandma looks over Mother's shoulder. "Yes, he does," she says quietly.

"Can I go, then? Can I check on her?"

"If you hurry," Mother says.

I dash over to Mrs. Osthoff's house and knock several times on the back door. Then I run around to the front of the house and do the same. I call through the open window, "It's me, Mrs. Osthoff. Helen." But there is no answer. She has retreated back inside herself.

I burst through our back door, out of breath. "She's not answering," I say. "We have to do something."

"I'm sure she's fine." Grandma hands me my lunch sack. "Hurry, now. You'll miss your train."

I look up at her helplessly. "Maybe we should ask her to stay with us for a few days. Just until things blow over."

Grandma's shoulders droop. She looks tired. "How about this?" she says. "I'll check on her later today, and I'll call Mr. Anderson and have him order a new windowpane."

"But why can't she stay here? She's probably

scared."

"Oh Helen, Eva is perfectly capable of taking care of herself. She's been doing it for years now. I'll check on her. You just go. Get to work."

I'm still worrying about Mrs. Osthoff and hoping Grandma sticks to her word when I arrive at work. I'm angry with myself for not telling Mrs. Osthoff what the people in town have been saying. It wouldn't have stopped those boys from throwing the rock through her window, but at least it wouldn't have come as such a surprise to her when they did. I'm wondering why it is that even when I try to do the right thing, I never quite get it all the way right.

When the line starts moving, I bring my attention back to my work, but it soon becomes clear that Martha is bent on causing trouble today. She can't seem to hold onto the timing devices. She drops them so often it puts us all behind. By lunchtime I'm furious, and I don't even have Janie with whom to vent my anger. So when Martha ruffles my hair as she passes, I drop my half-finished sandwich back in the bag and do something I never thought I'd have the guts to do. I march right out the front door of Westclox and across the street to the main office and ask to see a supervisor. One of the office girls takes me upstairs and knocks on the door of a Mr. Kopek. He's sitting behind a desk piled high with ledgers and files, but he stands up when I come into the room.

As soon as I sit down opposite him, though, I lose my nerve.

"How can I help you?" he asks, but I can't answer. He settles back in his chair. "I see," he says. "That bad, huh? Well, if it's something I need to know, I sure hope you'll find the voice to tell me."

I let out my breath and start talking, my words rushing over each other like kids playing leapfrog. I tell him all about Martha and Betty and how they try to slow down the line and about Mr. Mueller and how he's never around to make them stop and how I'm just trying to do my best and get my job done.

"Well, I guess you found your voice," Mr. Kopek says, coming around to sit on the corner of his desk. "You know, I gave a commendation to a girl not much older than you the other day. She had found more faulty parts than anyone else on her line. She was scared when I came to talk to her. It had been explained to her, of course, that every rejected piece costs this company money. She thought I was coming to tell her she was doing her job a little too well. Of course I wasn't happy about the money we were losing, but the fact is many of our Westclox boys have enlisted in the service now. If we don't make our products well, we endanger their lives. I want to see each and every one of them come home alive. I can get my wish if girls like you keep working as hard as you can." He takes my arm and draws me gently to my feet. "I appreciate you telling me your troubles, young lady. I'll look into it."

I'm stunned as I walk back down the wide staircase of the office building and across 5th Street. I hadn't expected to actually see a supervisor, much less be heard, much less be praised. I'm feeling pretty proud of myself as I take my seat back on the line and excited to see what will happen next.

"What're you grinnin' about?" Martha asks, but I don't answer her.

In fact, I ignore her for the rest of the day.

12

Nothing Easy

A week passes before Mrs. Osthoff lets me in again one evening after supper. I apologize for not telling her what people were saying about her, but she just stands there hugging herself and doesn't answer. She does agree, however, to let me call Mr. Anderson so he can fix the window the next day, and that gives me hope. I promise her I'll come over after work to see how it turned out.

But when I get home from work the next day, something unexpected is waiting for me. It's Janie, sitting on the tree swing, her feet stretched out in front of her, her hands gripping the ropes. She smiles at me shyly when I come through the gate. I walk over to her slowly, looking down at my shoes.

"Guess what?" she says.

"What?"

"I got a letter from John Beaumont."

My head snaps up. "You did? My aunt only just got one herself! What did he say?"

She stands up. "He called me 'My dear Janie' and said I was sweet to write to him. Why don't you come over to my house and read it? You can help me think up a reply."

I look at her sideways. "So you're not mad at me anymore?"

"I am a little. But I miss you too. All Maxine talks about is clothes."

I laugh, and Janie laughs with me. My heart is so full it's fit to burst. "Come inside," I say. "I have to tell Mother where I'm going."

"Ask her if you can spend the night."

"But I have to get up so early for work," I say.

"That's all right. I'll walk you to the train in the morning."

I can't believe she's offering such a thing. Janie hates getting up early. So now I know she truly has forgiven me. I'm giddy with excitement as I rush inside to tell Mother. It seems like so long since Janie and I have been together, and it seems like yesterday.

We have so much to talk about! It's good to have my best friend back.

The next day at work, I'm feeling happy, though a little tired. Janie and I stayed up way too late talking about John and Maxine and all the things that had been going on that summer. I told her about Mrs. Osthoff, and only then did I remember I'd promised to look in on her. I'll do it this evening, as soon as I get home from work.

It's unbearably hot in the factory today, and that has put Martha in a worse mood than usual. Nothing has changed in the past week. At first, I kept looking around for Mr. Kopek, expecting him to show up and reprimand Martha and Betty. From what I can tell, though, no one has talked to them, and Mr. Mueller is still nowhere to be seen.

I guess I shouldn't have gotten my hopes up so high. Maybe in the end, my conversation with Mr. Kopek was nothing more than a little girl complaining about some bullies. I'm embarrassed now that I took up his time that way. A man as busy as that has bigger things to worry about than a little teasing on one of his production lines.

By lunchtime, I'm sweaty and exhausted. After I eat, I head over to the drinking fountain and the salt tablet dispenser that sits beside it. The tablets dissolve quickly in your mouth and supposedly help prevent that heat lag that drags you down as the day wears on. Rita joins me at the drinking fountain, dabbing some water on her forehead and the back of her neck.

"Did you hear about Mr. Mueller?" she asks.

"No, what?"

"He's been fired."

My chest tightens as I wait for her to continue.

"Someone told on him, that he doesn't walk the line like he's supposed to. So they've been keeping an eye on him. He's been gambling in the men's room, but what's worse, he's been keeping black market sugar in the storage room. Apparently he sells it from there to pay off his gambling debts. One of the supervisors called him down last night and fired him."

"Mr. Kopek," I say excitedly, feeling proud of my role in catching a dirty crook. But Rita just cocks her head.

"How do you know that? Was it you who told on him, Helen?"

"Not just him. Martha and Betty too. Why are you looking at me like that, Rita? We've all been wanting things to change. I just decided to do something about it."

Rita takes me by the arm and leads me over to a table. Ever since she got married, she's been acting more like my mother than my friend, and I don't like it. I yank my arm away, but I sit down with her anyway, and she puts her head close to mine.

"Maybe you shouldn't have said anything, Helen."

"Why not?! Don't you want to win this war? Don't you think we should all be doing our jobs? Our best jobs?"

"Of course, but it's more complicated than that. Mr. Mueller has a wife and two little boys. The youngest is sickly. They have lots of medical bills, and with Mr. Mueller in jail, who's to pay them? If his wife takes a job, who's to watch their sons?"

"Well, I didn't know that!"

"I know. I just think maybe you should have kept matters to yourself."

"You certainly should have," Martha says. I hadn't noticed her sneaking up behind Rita.

Betty moves alongside her. Rita stands, making a kind of barrier between me and Martha, but Martha just pushes her aside and leans down into my face. "We know it was you who told on us. We got called down to Mr. Kopek's office last night same as Mueller. Kopek laid it on the line. Said we better get our acts together, or we'll be out on our fannies. You've got some nerve, little girl."

"I'm not a little girl," I say, standing up so I can look down on Martha instead of her looking down on me. "I didn't mean to get Mr. Mueller fired, but I wouldn't have minded one bit if he'd fired you." My heart is beating so hard I can feel it in my throat. I've never spoken like this to someone older than me before, and now a few of the women from our line have noticed that something is going on and have gathered around, which makes me even more nervous. I'm not at all sure what to do next. I don't trust my decisions anymore. It seems like every course of action I've taken this summer has reaped bad results. Even in this case, I did what I thought was right, but now I'm the one being criticized. I want to give up and run home, but I don't, mainly because it's Martha and I've had my fill of her. I stand my ground, waiting to see what she will do next.

"You think I'm lazy, don't you, girl? Well I'm not. I could work as hard as a young thing like you any day."

"Then why don't you?"

"You just wait, little miss. When you've been here as long as I have, you'll learn to pace yourself too," she says, her voice rising. "You'll learn to take things one minute at a time. It's the only way you'll make it through another sorry day."

I'm surprised to see tears in Martha's eyes, the same kind that are rising in mine, tears of anger and frustration and a little bit of hurt.

"Ah, leave it alone, Martha," Betty says. "She'll be goin' back to school in a few weeks and that'll be the end of it. Come on now." She reaches for Martha, but Martha pulls away.

"You stay clear of me," she says, wagging her finger in my face.

I want to say something strong or brave or even witty, but all that comes out as they walk away is, "How am I supposed to do that?"

Rita puts her hand on my shoulder. "Don't worry," she says, "I'll find someone who's willing to switch places with you on the line. We'll get you farther away from those two."

I don't want to accept her help. I want to handle this on my own, but I can't think of a better solution than the one Rita has offered, and I certainly can't stomach the idea of sitting between Martha and Betty for the rest of the summer. I watch Rita go off to talk to the other women and feel their eyes on me as they discuss the situation. I sink back down on the chair and consider going to the medical center to tell them I'm sick. I want to get out of the factory, but I don't want to go home. I don't want to face my family and tell them once again how I've bungled everything. I could hang out by the lake until dinnertime or stay in LaSalle and visit the shops downtown. Anything sounds better than going back into that assembly room and taking my place at the line.

So that's what I do. I take myself down to the medical clinic and tell the nurse I have a terrible stomachache, which isn't exactly a lie. I do feel sick about what happened and about how cowardly I'm behaving now. But it feels good to punch my time card out and walk through those double doors into the fresh air. I'm too afraid to go window-shopping, concerned someone from the factory will see me, and I don't want to go back to Hayden's Valley just yet. What I'd like to do is head over to the swimming pool, where so many kids are whiling away the summer. I want to do what the other kids are doing, something that won't make me have to think, but I don't have my swimsuit, and I'm afraid of being seen. I can think of nothing else, so I reluctantly catch the bus home. As I'm walking down the back alley, I hear voices—boys' voices—yelling with excitement.

I run ahead, but when I get to Mrs. Osthoff's house, I stop cold. Stanley Fuller and a couple of others boys are standing on Mrs. Osthoff's roof pulling down her weather vane. In the yard below, several kids are watching, including Janie. And from a side window, peeking through the curtains, Mrs. Fuller is watching too.

"Stop it!" I scream, picking up a rock and throwing it at the boys. "Leave her alone."

"It's okay, Helen," Janie says, running up and catching my arm. "Mrs. Osthoff's gone."

I stare at her. "What do you mean gone?"

"Mrs. Fuller saw her board the westbound train earlier today. She was carrying a suitcase. She's gone."

I rush to Mrs. Osthoff's kitchen window, stepping on the back row of carrots in order to see fully into the kitchen. The counters are clear, and the cupboard doors are closed tight. I run around to the front of the house, Janie following, and cup my hands around the front window. The furniture is covered in sheets. All the pictures are off the walls and off the side table in the hallway too. I try the doorknob, but it's locked. I slam my fist against the door.

"I can't believe she left," I say. "It's because of me. I was supposed to see her last night, but I was with you."

"I'm sure that's not it," Janie says.

"You don't understand. All summer I've been trying to prove how responsible I could be, and all I've done is make mistakes. I waited too long to tell you about Hal, and now he's gone. I got Mr. Mueller fired, and now Martha hates me more than ever. And I broke my promise to Mrs. Osthoff. Every time I've tried to do the right thing, I've made things worse."

"You didn't know she'd leave," Janie says, stroking my arm. Just then the weather vane hits the ground in front of the house, and Stanley jumps down off the roof with a jubilant shout.

"Leave me alone, okay, Janie?" I sink down on the porch and pull my knees to my chest, watching Stanley and the other boys carry the weather vane over to Stanley's house. Janie hesitates, but when she sees I'm not going to budge, she runs behind the house. I sit by myself, my back against Mrs. Osthoff's house, my chin buried between my knees, not even bothering to wipe away the tears.

A few minutes later I hear the click of heels on the walkway that circles the house. Grandma Kate appears.

"Helen?" she says, standing over me. I stare straight ahead.

"So that's how it's going to be, huh?" she says. "All right then." She gathers her dress around her legs and lowers herself to the porch beside me. She stretches her legs out straight and looks across the dry front yard, her arms crossed over her chest. The Miller boy rides up and down on his bicycle, waving as he passes, and we watch him in silence. She can wait me

115

out, I know it. She's done it before. So I give up my pouting and speak.

"Did Janie tell you I was here?"

"She did."

"Did you know Mrs. Osthoff had gone?" I ask finally.

"Not until this afternoon. Mrs. Fuller told me."

"It's my fault."

"Is it now?"

"I promised I'd check in on her last night, and I didn't."

"Oh I think there's more than enough blame to go around."

I turn my head to look at her, wiping my tears on the back of my arm. She lays a hand on my knee. "Helen, I spent years trying to get that woman out of her house, and then I guess I just gave up. But things were different lately, and I should have taken note of that. You tried to tell me, but I didn't listen, did I?"

"We should have done more for her," I say stubbornly.

Grandma Kate leans her head back against the house and sighs. "You're right. I've just been so tired this summer taking care of the house and the garden and all of you. I didn't think I had the strength to care for one more person, so I left her to care for herself. So there you have it," she says, nudging me. "I made a poor decision."

She reaches into her dress pocket and pulls out a handkerchief that's folded into a neat square and hands it to me. I unfold it slowly, noticing the sharp creases where she'd ironed it closed and the delicate initials she had stitched into the corner. I open the handkerchief and wipe my eyes.

"Did you think it was only children who made mistakes?" Grandma asks.

I don't answer immediately. As always, she has guessed exactly what I'm thinking. "Grown-ups make them too," she goes on. "The only difference between a grown-up's mistake and a child's is the size of the consequence. I thought Eva would go on as she always had. I was wrong. A pretty big mistake, and now I'll have to live with it."

"I thought it would be easy this summer," I say. "Making the right decisions. Showing you how responsible I could be. But it all gets so . . . complicated. Life just feels too big sometimes. Like the war. I need one of Grandpa's maps with pins telling me where to go next."

Grandma Kate pats my knee. "You've no need for a map, Helen. You're doing just fine on your own, and I'm proud of you."

The Miller boy comes by again on his bike. He stops and asks us what we're doing.

"We're catching flies," Grandma Kate says. "Run along now. We're very busy."

The Miller boy cocks his head and gives us a quizzical look, then shrugs with all his body, as only a child of five can do. I have to laugh as he rides away.

"You're feeling better then?" Grandma Kate asks.

"A little."

"Good, then help an old woman up. This floor is much too hard on my bones."

I stand and stretch out my hand. "You're not old, Grandma."

"No? I just feel old then." She puts her arm around my waist. At the foot of the stairs, I pivot to look back once more at Mrs. Osthoff's house.

"Where do you think she's gone, Grandma? She can't go home to Germany. There's a war on."

"I don't know, Helen. She always talked about California. When Frederick was little, she used to tell

118

him she'd take him swimming in the ocean someday. He used to paint pictures of the sea. He was a fine painter. When he left, I always wondered if he went there. If he set up a life for himself where he could watch the sun set over the water. Maybe he had a place there. Maybe that's where she went."

"Do you think she'll come back?"

"I hope so, dear. I really do."

13

The Barn Dance

It's a Saturday night in late August, and my family is heading across the river for a barn dance. Grandpa ran into Mr. Russell in town the other day. He owns a farm not far from where Grandpa's land used to be. His son Jimmy is home on leave, and the dance is in his honor. Mr. Russell has invited us to come! Janie's coming too. I haven't been this excited for anything since my first day of work at Westclox.

Tonight is our last hurrah in the car. Grandpa George wants to take it out one last time before he donates the tires to the rubber drive and puts the car on blocks for the duration of the war. Grandma tried to talk him out of it, but Grandpa said, "Come, now, Kate. Let an old man do *something* to help the war effort," and that took the fight right out of her. We had to borrow gas coupons from the Breys to make it all the way out to the Russells and back, but Grandpa says it'll be worth it.

So here I sit in the middle of the wide, rear seat of our Oldsmobile with Mother on my left, fussing with her lapel pin, and Janie on my right. Janie borrowed that navy blue dress from Maxine—the one that Mrs. Land said I was too tall to wear—and of course it looks good on her. I'm wearing a hand-me-down dress from my cousin. It's a little out-of-date now, but it's actually quite pretty. It's a misty rose color with two rows of flower buttons down the bodice and a tie-back sash, but the best part is the pleated skirt—perfect for dancing. Janie came over early to help me curl my hair, and a couple of carefully placed barrettes are hiding the spot where it was torn out by the drill. Janie has forbidden me to touch my hair. She keeps grabbing my hand whenever I start to smooth it down out of habit. She says she won't have all her hard work ruined.

There's a small, black handbag resting on Janie's lap, and she's laid her hands over it protectively. Inside she has a lipstick, a small mirror, some extra hairpins and, most importantly, her latest letter from John. My family has received a few letters from him too, so we now know for certain he's in Britain. Grandpa says John will be flying some very dangerous missions, and the weather over the English Channel can be treacherous. We are tracking the Air Force movements as best we can on the map, but not even that eases our worry much. His letters help, though, which is why I made Janie swear to tell me as soon as she gets one.

"Okay," she said. "But I can't let you read them anymore."

"Why not!"

"Because they're personal."

"That's silly, Janie. He's my cousin."

"Well, he's my beau now. Sort of. He said the girls in England are very nice, but not nearly as pretty as me. I'm going to send him a picture of me so he can carry it with him when he flies."

"Oh nausea," I say.

I can't begrudge her not sharing her letters, though. I got a letter myself that I haven't told Janie about. It was from Hal. He sent it just before he shipped out, and he thanked me for not giving away his secret. He said he'd been sure I would try to stop him from leaving, but he was glad I didn't. "This is where I belong, Lanie," he wrote. "I know that now more than ever." I'll have to tell him someday that I didn't mean to keep his secret, it just happened. But I won't do it now. If anything happens to Hal, I want him to know I'm his friend and always will be. I don't want him to doubt that for a minute.

I'm wondering where in the war Hal will wind up when Janie elbows me and asks, "Hey, how was your last day of work?"

I smile. After Rita found a woman to switch places with me earlier this month, and I got some distance between Martha and Betty, things got better. Martha still made fun of my new pageboy hairstyle one afternoon, but other than that, she kept mostly to herself. Maybe that had something to do with the new supervisor who seemed to be keeping a close eye on those two.

"Rita was sweet," I say. "She said she was going to miss me. Oh, and she promised to come and see me sing in the school operetta."

"And what about Martha?"

"Martha puffed up her chest and said, 'Good riddance, little girl.'"

"What'd you do?"

"I screwed up my courage and looked her straight in the eye. 'Oh you're not rid of me yet,' I said. 'I'll be back next year.' Oh Janie, I wish you could have seen the look on Martha's face!"

Janie laughs. "Serves her right, the old cow." She glances at Mother, and mumbles, "Sorry, Mrs. Marshall."

"Never mind, Janie. From what you girls have told us, 'old cow' probably suits that woman quite well. I wouldn't have minded giving her a piece of my mind this summer, but Helen seemed to have things well under control." She gives me a squeeze, and it's good to feel her arms around me again now that the casts have been removed.

"Here we are," Grandpa says, pulling the car into the field and parking. There are plenty of other cars and pick-up trucks and even a few wagons parked there already, and it's still early. I bet half the county is coming. I push Janie out of the car ahead of me and start whispering to her about who all we might see inside, until Grandma Kate gives me one of her looks. Whispering is something she cannot abide. "If you've got something to say, say it so everyone can hear," she says.

"Sorry, Grandma Kate." I glance at Janie, trying not to laugh.

As soon as everyone is out of the car, we walk down toward the barn, where the band is already tuning their instruments. Grandpa George says Mr. Russell brought the band all the way from LaSalle just for tonight, and I can't wait to hear them. At the church dances in Hayden's Valley, all we have are fiddlers and Mr. Hollis, who plays the accordion. I can't wait to hear this city band with their horns and drum set. Evidently I'm not the only one. There's a steady stream of cars heading down the dirt road, some of them honking their horns, which sets the cows bawling in the corral nearby.

At the entrance to the barn, there's a long, wooden table set up with bowls of punch and plates of molasses cookies with a little sign beside them that reads Only One Per Person Please. You never would have seen a sign like that before the war.

"Come on," Janie says. "Let's get one now before they're all gone."

She eats hers right away; so does Grandpa George. Grandma Kate passes. She's never had much of a sweet tooth anyway. Mother says she'll pass too, but then changes her mind and snatches a cookie off the plate with a sheepish grin. I decide to savor mine. I take a little bite and hold it in my mouth, letting it melt on my tongue, tasting the full flavor as Janie and I walk through the big barn doors.

The machinery has been parked out behind the barn and the dirt floor swept clean. There are hay bales stacked two deep in a U-shape around the center of the barn and more placed carefully just within each of the cleaned-out stalls. The band is set up on a raised platform near the front of the barn, and there's just enough room to dance within the U. In fact, there are already a few couples milling around inside it practicing their steps and waiting for the music to start. There's a gaggle of girls standing just inside the U on the far end, their heads together chattering excitedly, and a handful of teenage boys standing behind the hay bales, hands stuffed in their front pockets, watching the girls. And just inside the door, off to the right, there's a young man in a marine's uniform whom everyone keeps clapping on the back as they come in. It must be the Russell boy. He's talking to two girls a bit older than Janie and me, but he doesn't seem to favor one over the other. I can see Janie has noticed him too. She may be smitten with John, but John's a long way away tonight, and Janie's not about to pass up on a little fun. When Grandpa leads us over to greet the Russells, Janie tilts her head just slightly to the right and gives Jimmy Russell one of her prettiest smiles, and he can't help smiling back. Before we turn away, Jimmy makes Janie promise to save him a dance.

Grandpa goes off to find the other men to talk crops and the weather and the war. Grandma and Mother take a seat on a hay bale on the outside circle, sipping the punch they brought in with them from outside. Janie and I are too excited to sit. We stand behind the bale, eyeing the group of girls gathered in the back. They are eyeing us too. I smooth the pleats of my skirt self-consciously and reach to pat my hair, but Janie pulls my hand down. A murmur of excitement stirs the room as the local auctioneer takes to the makeshift stage and announces that the music will begin. The band comes on loud and strong, and the dancers push up close to the stage, their feet kicking up a fine dust.

Just then, a young marine circles the outside

of the U, heading right toward us. We all see him coming. We hadn't expected any other soldiers here tonight. He nods to the adults and smiles at Janie, but it's me he speaks to. The first thing I notice about him is that he's tall, very tall. He says his name is Paul Ellis, and he asks if I'd like to dance. I glance at Mother for permission.

"Yes, yes, go!" she says.

Paul takes my hand and leads me into the U. The dance is a jitterbug, my favorite, and as we jump and hop around the floor, I step on his foot only once. It's hot in the barn, and the scent of women's perfume and men's hair tonic mixes with the aroma of freshly cut hay and the smells of animals. There are sounds of happiness all around us, whoops and hollers from the dancers, shouts of encouragement from the audience, someone shooting off a gun outside in celebration. Paul asks me for another dance and then another, and only when I'm thoroughly out of breath do I pull him off to the side to rest.

"What brings you here?" I ask when my breath returns.

"Jimmy. We met at basic training. I'm from a little town just west of Chicago. I hitched a ride up here for the party."

"Where you stationed?" I'm looking somewhere just over his shoulder, so I don't have to meet his eye.

"We're shipping out for the Pacific," he says. "Jimmy and me." He leans his elbow on a stall railing and grins. "You're a good kid," he says. "You remind me of my little sister."

I look away so he won't see my disappointment. It's not exactly what I want to hear, of course. I search out Janie on the dance floor. She's not faring much better than me. She's doing a basic foxtrot with a boy we know from Hayden's Valley, and it's clear by the look on her face she's not anxious to dance with him again. She nods me toward the other side of the U and makes her excuses to the boy.

"I need to go now," I say to Paul.

"How 'bout a dance later? There aren't many girls tall enough to dance with me."

"Sure," I say, and dash over to where Janie is waiting for me. She holds out her hands and pulls me in to ask me what my soldier was like.

"He thinks I'm a kid," I say, rolling my eyes. "But he's a good enough dancer, I guess."

"You should offer to write to him," Janie suggests.

"Lots of girls are writing to the soldiers. It cheers them up to get mail."

"Maybe," I say, watching Paul saunter over toward Jimmy, and I might just do it. The troop trains are coming more and more often through our valley now. There will be lots more soldiers like Paul just passing through on their way to battle, and some of them, like Frederick, won't come home. If I can do something to make them feel better, maybe I will. If any of us had taken that sort of interest in Frederick, maybe Mrs. Osthoff never would have left.

I look for Mrs. Osthoff every night, but it's been a month since she left, and still her house remains dark and silent. Before Mrs. Osthoff, I thought war casualties were only the people who died or were injured in the fighting. Now I know that in one way or another, we are all touched by the war. A couple of weeks ago, we held a memorial service in our parlor for Frederick Osthoff. We had no body to bury, but Grandma Kate said it didn't seem fitting not to honor him in some way. She said we should have done something when we first heard the news. Several of the neighbors came to pay their respects. I had each of them sign a journal with their condolences, and I keep it in the top drawer of my dresser in case Mrs. Osthoff returns. We eat the produce that I've been growing in her little patch of garden, and come fall I'll dig it up and turn the soil in case she ever wants to use it again. I guess I'm still hoping she'll come home someday.

"What's the matter?" Janie asks. "You look sad."

"I was just thinking about Mrs. Osthoff, hoping she's all right."

"Oh no you don't," Janie insists. "There'll be no melancholy moods tonight. School starts on Monday. Summer's over. This is our last chance to let loose. Come on, let's dance."

She pulls me back onto the dance floor, and we dance together, with me leading, until our feet hurt. Then we collapse onto the hay bale next to Mother and Grandma Kate, slipping off our shoes and rubbing our feet.

"It's good to see you having a little fun, my sweet," Mother says.

"Yes, you've had a lot on your mind this summer," Grandma Kate adds. "You'll get a bit of a breather now that school is starting again."

I lean against her and smile. Now that I know

how much I can accomplish when I set my mind to it, I have no intention of slowing down. I'm no longer scared of the war. Now I just want to do my part. I'll be busy with homework and rehearsals for the operetta soon, but some of the kids and I are going to organize a war bonds drive at the school, and Grandma is showing me how to knit so I can help with the socks and mufflers. Janie has suggested we set up a map at school like the one Grandpa hung in the hallway to help the students better track the war. I think that's a good idea.

And from time to time I'll still stand at my window and close my eyes and try to feel John and Hal and even Mrs. Osthoff. It's childish, I know, to think I could actually know if something had happened to them, but that's okay. At the beginning of the summer, all I cared about was proving how grown up I could be. Now I have nothing to prove. There's a place for all of us in this war.

Meet the real Helen Marshall
Shirley Brand

Shirley Brand grew up an only child in a small town called DePue, Illinois. It was very much like my fictional town of Hayden's Valley. Like Helen, Shirley was very tall, and she did sing in operettas at school. She was often given the part of the mother because of her height. She was a good student when she wanted to be. Her mother worked hard in the town's zinc plant. It was her goal to send Shirley to college. But it's true that Shirley did work at Westclox in the summer and, at one point, made more money than her mother! And it's true the first thing she bought with her paycheck was a Mixmaster for her grandmother.

Shirley had three close cousins who went to war. One was killed; the other two made it home. One of her friends had a brother who joined the service. He was the inspiration for Hal in *Doing My Part*. And Mrs. Osthoff was loosely based on a real person who lived across the alley from Shirley, a woman who spoke little English and often wailed for her beloved son who'd gone off to war. It was Shirley's family who later had to deliver the message about this boy's death to his heartbroken mother.

And what about Westclox? What was it really like for Shirley? Very much as I described it in the book, including the accident with the drill and women like Martha and Betty who made things challenging for the younger girls.

Shirley is now eighty years old. She taught kindergarten for thirty-eight years and loves children. She lives in Colorado and is pleased to have a book based on her experiences.

If You'd Been Friends with Helen Marshall

If you'd been friends with Helen Marshall, you might have:

Helped her in her VICTORY GARDEN. During World War II, more than twenty million families planted Victory Gardens. Many, like Helen's, chose to expand gardens they already had. They planted familiar vegetables like tomatoes, carrots and lettuce, but also ones they'd never heard of before, like Swiss chard. Growing their own produce helped families deal with wartime food shortages and enabled them to save money they could donate to the war effort. People in cities planted gardens on the roofs of their high-rise buildings or in vacant lots. Even movie stars were proud to show off their Victory Gardens. At the end of the growing season, you and Helen may have helped your mothers "can" or "jar" the produce you had grown, so you could enjoy it all winter long.

Traded RATIONING STAMPS. Many foods were rationed during World War II to make sure the government had enough supplies and materials to meet its wartime needs. This meant that average families like Helen's had to keep track of the amount of meats, dairy products and sugar they used, among other things. They could purchase those items only if they had the correct amount of stamps or tokens. Not only food was rationed. Shoes, gasoline and women's nylon stockings were also controlled. Sometimes you could trade with a neighbor. Shirley Brand's family used to trade gasoline ration stamps to a dairy farmer, who gave them whipped cream in return.

Set up a WAR BONDS DRIVE. During World War II, Americans were encouraged to buy War Bonds, which were essentially a loan to the government so it could pay for the war. Even school children were asked to raise money to purchase bonds. Teachers would hand out Savings Bond booklets, and kids could purchase 10-cent or 25-cent Defense Stamps to paste into their booklets. When the booklet was filled, the child received a Savings Bond. American children like Helen raised over a *billion* dollars' worth of stamps and bonds to help win the war.

Handed out food to the TROOP TRAINS. When you and Helen were a little older, you might have gone with other high school girls to the nearby town of Streater to meet the troop trains traveling west from Chicago. Volunteers would gather at the depot to hand out coffee, sandwiches, cookies and fruit to the hungry troops passing through. Shirley Brand remembers passing coffee and doughnuts up through the train windows to the smiling servicemen.

Second in the Home-Front Heroes Series

The No-No Boys

Fourteen-year-old Tai Shimoda's family has lost everything. Like many other Japanese-Americans at the start of World War II, Tai's family has been forced to leave their home and move to Tule Lake Relocation Center in Northern California. Though he misses his friends back home, Tai does his best to start a new life behind the barbed wire of camp. But in the spring of 1943, tensions at Tule Lake are growing. Tai's older brother has joined a group that has refused to swear allegiance to the United States. They call themselves the No-Nos. Tai's father calls them Disloyals. When the camp begins to split in two, Tai must decide what *he* believes. Will he join his beloved brother and the No-Nos or, like his father, remain true to America?

About the Author

Teresa R. Funke writes for children and adults. Most of her books and short stories are based on real people and actual events, and many are set in World War II. She says, "I wrote *Doing My Part* to show my readers how important children were to winning that war. Everyone from President Roosevelt on down was asking for children's help. As Mrs. Land says in the book, it must have been an exciting time to be a kid."

Teresa also enjoys teaching new writers as a popular presenter and writers' coach, but what she likes best is spending time with her husband and three children at their home in Colorado. She'd love it if you visited her website at www.teresafunke.com to submit your own family's stories from World War II or other time periods, or to invite Teresa to speak at your school.